# Honey

a spirited child who became
an extraordinary woman

## CLAIRE "HONEY" GILBERT

iUniverse, Inc.
New York   Bloomington

Honey
a spirited child who became an extraordinary woman

iUniverse books may be ordered through booksellers or by contacting:

iUniverse
1663 Liberty Drive
Bloomington, IN 47403
www.iuniverse.com
1-800-Authors (1-800-288-4677)

ISBN: 978-1-4401-7337-0 (pbk)
ISBN: 978-1-4401-7338-7 (ebk)

Printed in the United States of America

iUniverse rev. date: 9/18/2009

To my children, Alan and Jerry, who were always there when I needed them most and to my grandchildren, Brigette and Christopher, who I hope will find happiness and a good direction in what life holds for them.

I want to thank Barbara Pawley who walked through this book with me all the way and for all the editing, guidance and support she gave me. Every once in a while, a person is lucky enough to make an unforgettable friend: I thank Geraldine Randels for always being there as my friend.

# Part One

## CHILDHOOD

The fire in the old wood-burning cook stove was going good and Harry had gone out to the barn to do the farm chores. He had come downstairs to their farm-house style kitchen earlier, to get the fire started for Elsie to prepare breakfast for her family.

When Elsie came down, she immediately put the coffee on the stove for her and Harry and started breakfast for the family. When their two older boys had eaten, they were out the door in a hurry; Eddy was headed for his job and Bill to school.

Soon Harry came back in with an armload of wood and carrying a pail of water from the big, old pump in the yard. As he came up on the porch, he got a whiff of scrapple frying. He loved scrapple for breakfast. He had just made it the day before. It was slaughter time, and he always made scrapple when he butchered. It was made from the meat scraps, ground up and set in a mold to form a loaf, then sliced and fried. It was an old, Dutch recipe. Elsie delighted in cooking scrapple for Harry because she knew how much he loved it for breakfast. She was always happy to give him what he liked; he was such a good man, loving and considerate. She had loved him a long time.

As she cooked, her thoughts went back to their beginning.

They met when she was very young and he was just out of the Spanish – American War. They wanted to marry right away, but he thought it would be better to wait until he got a good job so he could have something better to offer her. At the present time he was playing around with wrestling and a few small boxing bouts. He was a stocky, little guy with huge shoulders and a thick chest. He hadn't quite made up his mind what he wanted to do. To make money he was competing in some wrestling and boxing matches. He was a feather-weight—short, but mighty.

Harry's family was very pleased that he wanted to marry Elsie Miller. They liked her a lot, but they were happy that Harry wanted to wait until he had a good job before he took on the responsibility of marriage. Elsie's family did not approve of Harry and gave her an ultimatum: Stop seeing him and don't plan on marrying him or find a new home. Elsie's mother was a tiny thing, but she had a very pompous way about her. She would not hear of their daughter marrying Harry Diehl, with his sparring bouts and no job. She had bigger plans for her. But Elsie could not see anyone but Harry; she loved him and wanted to marry him.

When she told Harry of her predicament, he said, "Don't worry, we'll talk to my mammy, maybe she'll talk to your folks and get it straightened out."

Mammy was Harry's mother. His dad had passed on two years earlier. Well, Mammy did talk to Elsie's parents, but it was to no avail. Mammy thought about it for awhile, and finally said to Harry, "We have that extra room off the back porch and Elsie could stay there."

So Elsie moved in with the Diehl family until she and Harry could get married. Harry found a good job driving a delivery wagon for the brewery company. He really wanted to get a job with the steel mill because that paid better, but he couldn't wait for that so he took the delivery job in the meantime.

Harry had worked as a water-boy at the steel mill when he was very young. At that time he carried water to the workers on the blast furnaces. It was a hot job, but he felt lucky to have the opportunity, being a young boy. That was before he was called to the war.

The wedding was a very nice one, but was held without Elsie's family. The Diehl family was a big one, so it made up for that. Harry was well respected by his family and those who knew him.

Elsie looked lovely. She was such a tiny thing, less than five feet tall. Harry used to tell how he could almost reach around her waist with his two hands. No one ever knew if that was true or not, but he did have large hands for such a short, stocky man. Harry looked so handsome in his new dark suit and bow tie, with his hair slicked down and his shoes so shiny they looked like patent leather. You could use them for a mirror. He had a great proud look on his face. It was such a joyful day.

Harry came into the kitchen and interrupted her thoughts of the wedding. "What's that delicious aroma I just got a big whiff of?" he asked as he put his arm around her. By that time he was really hungry. As he pulled out the chair to sit, they could hear their youngest, clomping down the back stairs. He was about six, a mischievous little guy always playing tricks and "spoofing," as Harry called it.

Elsie and Harry had two other boys at this time. They were older and out of the house earlier in the morning. William or "Bill," as he was called, was thirteen and selling papers after school. Eddy was sixteen and working, driving a truck. Another son, George, born between Bill and Ralph, died of pneumonia at eighteen months old.

Elsie started to pour Harry's coffee. As she poured, she watched Ralph sit down at the table, and she immediately ordered him back upstairs to brush his teeth. "And for goodness sake, comb that hair and put your shoes on."

In a very few minutes he was back at the table. He gobbled up his oatmeal and was out the door to meet his school buddy and the neighbor with the horse and buggy to take them to school.

Elsie gave a sigh of relief and sat down to join Harry with breakfast. Now, she thought, they could have a little peace and quiet. This was his day off, and she would enjoy being with him.

He was working at the steel mill now and his shifts alternated—one week days, one week nights, and one week swing. He was working on the blast furnaces, and that was hard work. He had been working on that job for about fifteen years by this time.

"Harry, I'm concerned about Eddy," she said as she reached over to refill his cup with coffee.

"Why?" Harry asked. "He's a good boy, what are you worrying about?"

"Well, he's been seeing that nurse, Anna, pretty regular and staying out pretty late at night, and I think they're getting real serious."

"So what's wrong with that?" Harry asked.

"Well, you know" she replied. "When they are together so frequently there is a possibility the girl may come up pregnant, and I don't want Eddy to bring any shame to the family."

"Ach, you worry too much," he replied in his Dutch accent.

All was quiet for a few minutes, and as Harry pushed his empty plate away he said, "You know, Elsie, I think we should sell this farm and move closer to town. This is too much work for you, and I don't have the time anymore with the livestock and butchering. We have raised the boys now pretty well out here. What do you think?"

"Oh yes," she exclaimed. "I've been thinking about that lately, too. In fact I saw a wonderful place for sale when we went in to the marketplace last time. It's over on Washington Street. It's a brick end unit of a row of houses. It's a nice two-story and it's close to school for the boys. I'd love it. You must see it Harry."

"Alright, we'll go and see it tomorrow," Harry promised.

They did go and looked it over. Both agreed they liked it and would move as soon as possible.

Elsie and Harry settled into their nice, two-story, brick house. A few years passed. Bill gave up his paper route for a better opportunity. While he was delivering papers one evening, one of his customers, Mr. Wilson, stopped him and asked if he would like to get a better job in the offices at the steel mill. Mr. Wilson was an executive with the steel mill and admired Bill's ambition.

Of course, Bill said, "Yes, but I'll ask my Dad first."

One evening, Mr. Wilson visited Harry and Elsie and made them an offer. He said to them, "If you folks would allow Bill to quit school, I'll put him into a business school and have him learn a special business course. After his course, I'll get him a position in the buyer's office at the steel mill." Elsie thought that was great, and she and Harry heartily agreed. They hadn't known of anyone who had gotten that good an offer. So Bill gave up the paper route and started business school.

All seemed to be well after the move. Elsie made a lot of friends, and she and Harry liked their neighbors.

Elsie loved the marketplace, which was much closer now. She did her shopping there every week—the prices were lower than at the regular grocer's. She liked to buy fresh oysters and clams when they were in season.

One day Elsie's neighbors asked her if she would bring some items back for them. Soon many neighbors were asking her for the same favor. Finally Elsie decided that if she was doing this she might as well convert her living room into a store.

She brought in oysters and clams, pickles by the barrel, and breads and candies. She got some display cases for the candies and other shelf items. The neighbors were very happy to have a convenient place to shop in their neighborhood.

So Elsie had her store.

Not long after that, when Harry came home from work one day, Elsie called out, "Harry, you must come here, I have news."

"Oh, what is it now?"

"Well, don't be shocked, but we are going to have another child."

"What!" Harry cried, "After all this time? I thought you were in the change and couldn't have any more. Are you sure?"

"Well, you know Harry, I've always wanted a little girl and maybe this time we'll be lucky, and I'll get my wish."

"So be it!" Harry strode into the front room and hugged Elsie. Elsie continued to be busy with her store, buying her goods at the marketplace and selling them to the neighbors.

One night during a very bad storm with lots of thunder and lightning, Elsie heard a terrible explosion and the sound of things crashing. When the noise died down, she went to see what it was and discovered that the house was struck by lightning. Harry was still at work, and Eddie and Bill were out with their girlfriends. Elsie was so frightened she didn't know what to do. There was a big hole in the wall in the upstairs bedroom, and all the brick on the exterior was gone. Rubble covered the room. With the help of little Ralph, they covered it up with some cardboard. This should last until Harry gets home and fixes it, she thought. Harry was working the graveyard shift and wouldn't be home 'til morning. The next morning, Harry called a contractor and had it fixed. Elsie was relieved.

It wasn't long after that incident that Elsie had her baby girl on a cold, snow-sleet night at about one o'clock in the morning. Eddy and Bill remembered because they had been to a party in Easton about ten miles from their home and didn't get home 'til late because of the storm.

They had all looked forward to this and hoped it would be a girl.

Elsie knew what she was going to name her. She had picked out a name long ago. She knew of a lady years before with the name of Claire, and she said then that if she ever had a girl she would like to name her Claire.

Well Harry and the boys did not agree to the name. They thought it was too old a name for a little girl. They decided right then that they would call her "Honey." That name stuck with the little girl through her childhood. She was the apple of her papa's and brothers' eyes. She was their "little Honey" and everyone called her Honey Diehl.

Elsie idolized her little girl. She would dress her, curl her hair, and play with her like she was a little doll.

A few years passed, Eddy and Bill got married and Eddy became a father, which meant that Honey had a niece very close to her own age.

After a year or so of running the store and caring for her family, Elsie began to feel the strain of it all. Harry noticed, and one day he told her to sit down. He wanted to talk to her. She looked puzzled.

"What is it?" she asked.

"Elsie we're going to give up this business. You've made a good living and been successful here, but you've had enough. I want to build you a little cottage, something just for you and me and Honey and Ralph.

Elsie welcomed his idea and she agreed. As luck would have it, there was a lot right on the next street just across from their store. Elsie thought that would be a great place for their new home. It was an open area with a couple of nice, big trees. The children could still go to the same school.

They sold the business and house and rented a place a short distance away while they built their new house. So it was that Elsie and Harry built their little cottage.

Honey can still remember the walks with Mama and Papa through the field to take them to the new home, carrying things Mama wanted to bring to the new house. Honey was about three and Mama allowed her to carry the small things. Honey was so little she could hardly see over the grass.

Honey still has some memories of that cottage. She loved to run up and down the back stairs to the bedrooms where she and Ralph slept—Mama's and Papa's bedroom was downstairs

She sat on a high stool in the kitchen on Sundays while Mama curled her hair before sending her to Sunday school. Mama used a curling iron heated in the coal-burning kitchen stove. Papa was outside washing and polishing his new, sporty Durant convertible sedan. He shined it until you could see yourself in it. Honey could watch him through the window while Mama did her hair. Honey was a tiny girl with soft chestnut brown hair and big dark brown eyes that seemed to pop out at you.

Her two older brothers visited them with their future wives, turning on the Victrola phonograph and dancing in the living room. They would have her stand on their shoes to dance with her—she loved that. She can even remember some of the songs that they danced to, and Papa sang along.

She recalls visiting Grammy Diehl (Papa's mama) at her little house in Lightsville with the closed-in porch in the back, off her kitchen and the pie safe full of freshly-baked pies ready for any visitors. Grammy always wanted visitors to feel welcome.

All was going very well. Elsie had the house she wanted and the little girl she always wanted; and Harry had the job he wanted. The two older boys were married, and Eddy had a little girl and Bills wife was expecting. Ralph, of course, was still at home and a mischievous teenager.

It was Monday. Elsie always washed on Mondays. It was a nice, sunny day and the clothes seemed to dry really fast, so she decided she would put the ironing board up in the kitchen and iron a few things. While she was ironing, she got a sudden, very peculiar feeling, as though she was going to faint. Things became a little fuzzy, and she reached for the back of a chair to steady herself. What's wrong, she thought to herself. I never had this feeling before. I'm not going to mention this to Harry; he will just worry about it. It's probably the menopause. She decided to just let it pass. She had noticed that her feet had been swelling a lot lately, though. She didn't mention that to Harry either.

Elsie did have cause for concern in the coming weeks. Her spells became more frequent. Soon she couldn't put it off any longer and she had to tell Harry who immediately called the doctor. The doctor came over to the house and after examining Elsie, ordered her to bed.

Elsie kept asking, "What is it Doctor? What is it Harry?"

"We'll have to see, Elsie, just stay in bed," said the doctor as he and Papa walked out the door to the living room.

"What do you think, Doc?" Harry asked.

"Well, I don't know yet, it looks to me like she has dropsy, but there could be something causing the edema."

"What's edema Doc?" Harry asked.

"Well, it's the retention of water in the system that the body tissues do not throw off, and you get swelling. It can cause many problems, especially with the kidneys. We don't know how long she's had this problem. It could be serious. I've ordered her to stay in bed and off her feet and drink lots of water. We may have to drain her if it gets any worse."

It did get worse. Honey remembers seeing the doctor and Papa carry out big pails of foamy liquid out of Mama's bedroom. She wondered what that was all about. It seemed that this went on for a long time.

The day that Elsie asked to have her little girl brought to her bedside was a day that Honey would never forget. It was indelibly imprinted in her little mind. Her papa took her by the hand and led her into the bedroom; he put his arm around her and lifted her up onto the bed next to her mama.

"What's wrong Mama? Your eyes look so funny." Though Honey was not quite five years of age, she could sense something was wrong.

Elsie gave a slight smile and said in a weak voice, "I'm going to go away, Honey, and I want you to be a good girl and mind your papa."

Honey nodded her head in agreement. Then her mama said to her papa, "I want you to put my diamonds in a safe deposit box and give them to her when she's sixteen." Papa agreed. Honey didn't understand then what all this meant. She was to learn that later. She scurried off the bed and back to her play in the back yard.

One day, not too long after that, as she was playing with her dolls and toys in the backyard, she looked up and saw a lot of people gathering in the house and yard. What's happening? She thought maybe Mama and Papa were having a party. What else could bring all these people and all those cars? Then she heard her papa calling her. He met her as she came around the corner of the kitchen and swooped her up in his arms.

"What Papa?" she asked.

"Honey, I want you to come and say bye-bye to your mama; she's going away. As he spoke he lifted her above a huge box, all shiny and ruffled and pretty. Mama looked so pretty lying there among all those ruffles, sleeping

"Your mama is going away and you won't see her again," he told her.

"No!" Honey screamed. "I don't want her to go away!" She cried and wriggled out of his arms to her feet. She started running to get away—she didn't know where, but she wanted to get away. She didn't like what was happening.

She began to run around the boxwood hedge that lined the front yard. People were trying to catch her, but she didn't want them to touch her. She kept running and crying and sobbing. "No! No!" She felt that she was losing part of herself, and she wanted to get away from that thought.

Finally one of her papa's brothers, Uncle Bill, picked her up and hugged her to him and she sobbed on his shoulder as he patted her to console her. She was never to forget the sight of the men carrying the big box, taking her mama away from her.

The rest of the day held nothing for her. It was a long time before another trauma made that big of an impression on her.

The days that passed brought many strange ladies to the house to be housekeepers and to care for Honey and Ralph. There were all different types of women. But one day Papa came home with a large buxom woman who was very attractive and much taller than Papa.

Honey was playing with some miniature doll furniture that her brother Bill's father-in-law had made for her. He was an invalid in a wheel chair, and this was a hobby of his. Everyone loved Honey and wanted to do nice things for her. He took great pleasure in making these miniature things for her. Honey loved them.

She heard her papa call to her, but she didn't obey him immediately, and soon he came and took her by the hand and led her to the living room where the woman was sitting. Who is this woman, Honey thought. Is she another housekeeper?

"Honey, this is the lady that's going to take care of you. Her name is Esther."

"I want my mama to take care of me, where is she?" Honey cried.

"She's not coming back, so I will take care of you, and you must mind me," the woman said.

Honey wasn't sure if she was going to like this woman. She ran out to the backyard under the big tree to play with her toys again.

Soon after, this woman brought home a pretty, little girl about one and half years old with long, blonde, curly hair. Papa said she was just big enough to come under the dining room table when she stood up. She was very pretty and shy. Honey was glad to have someone to play with, and she liked her. Her name was Elaine.

Papa began to take Esther out. Soon she came back with a beautiful, fur coat and another time, new jewelry, and so on. One day when they returned home, he said, "Honey, she's going to be your new mama." Honey learned later that he had married the big woman.

"Now you will have to call me Mother and not Esther anymore."

Honey had always heard her papa call her Esther, and Ralph called her Esther. That was her name as far as she knew. "But you're not my mama, and I can't call you Mama."

"We'll see," she retorted.

One day, Honey and Elaine were playing with the miniature toys. Esther came out and bent over them and said, "Claire," (she didn't like anyone calling Claire, "Honey") this is your little sister now and I'm your mother, and you must give all your toys to her."

If she had said, "You must share your toys with her," Honey would not have been so upset. Honey didn't know what to say. She just sat there under the tree and cried. She never got to play with her toys again.

For a long time Honey was in a quandary as to what was happening, so many things were changing. One day she heard Ralph and Esther having a big argument. It was over Ralph not calling her mother. Ralph said as far as he was concerned, she was not his mother, and he would never call her mother. He must have said something bad to her then, because when Papa came home, Papa and Ralph had a big fight, and Papa socked Ralph in the jaw. Papa had never lifted his hand to any of his children until then. After that, Ralph left home and never came back. He said he wouldn't come to that house as long as she was there.

Honey couldn't call Esther, Mother, either. She didn't call her anything. One day Esther said to Honey, "I want you to call me Mother when you speak to me."

Honey replied, "No, you're not my mother." Esther gave her a swift slap in the face and said, "You get in that stairwell and stay until you decide to do what I say, you little bitch."

Honey sat in that stairwell in the dark all day. When her papa came home, Esther called her and said, "You may come out of there now." Her papa didn't know Honey had been there all day.

Life went on like that. Then Honey heard Papa and Esther talking about bringing some boys to live with them. She had two boys by her previous marriage who were living in Ohio somewhere, and she wanted to bring them to Papa's house

And they did come. Perry was five years old and Fred was eight.

Many tears were shed by Honey because she was not allowed to do what the others did. She was too young to understand the whole situation.

Honey seemed to get along with the other children; she had no problems with them. Perry always came to Honey's defense when Esther scolded or punished her for something. If they were on an outing and the children wanted an ice cream, they could ask for chocolate, but Honey wasn't permitted to ask; she just got strawberry. Honey didn't like strawberry, so it would end up in the garbage and she would get none. Then she cried.

Although the other children received toys, it seemed that Honey didn't get any. Maybe she was supposed to share. But the boys got boys' toys, which were not right for Honey, and Elaine's toys weren't big enough for Honey.

When Honey was almost six years old, it was time to go to school. The school was not far from the cottage. The time seemed to go by, and Honey met new chums to play with.

At first, the kids made fun of her because she wore Long John underwear and high-topped, laced shoes. They called them funny shoes. Sometimes Claire hated to go home, but if she was a little late she got a spanking with the strap and privileges restricted and usually had to stay in the house.

One night when she returned home from school, she was studying spelling and Esther told her to spell "cat." Honey was a little nervous and spelled it with an "s," although she meant to say "c." And she kept saying "s" instead of "c" over and over again. Every time she would get a slap in the face, and she would cry harder and harder. Between the sobs and the slaps, she kept on spelling "sat." She didn't think she was wrong. In her mind she was thinking "c" but saying "s." When Esther finally showed her what she was doing, she understood. All she had to do was show her the mistake.

When honey was in the second grade, the music teacher discovered that she could carry a tune so she made her practice, and she coached her. When the school staged a children's operetta called *HMS Pinafore*, the teacher asked if she would like to sing in it. Honey was delighted to hear that someone thought she was good enough. She almost flew home to ask if she could be in it. When she first asked Esther, she was told "no" because the boys were not included. Of course, Honey cried. But when Papa came home, Honey told him about it, and he talked to Esther, and then he told her she could do it.

Honey performed in the operetta and sang "Dear Little Buttercup," and did very well. After that, she got the opportunity to perform in another one and sang "Let It Snow, Let it Snow." It was a winter play, close to Christmas time. Honey really loved to sing and would sing whenever no one was there to make fun of her.

Later, there was the day that Esther planned to take all the kids somewhere. Honey did something that made Esther angry, and she slapped Honey, saying, "Now you are not going with us, you can just stay here by yourself until we come back." And she locked the house up so Honey couldn't go out. At that time, Honey was a little more than six years old.

After they were gone, Honey climbed up on a chair and up on top of the old-fashioned icebox and out of the window above. Then she jumped down to the ground outside. All she could think of was to get away. Where would she go? Then she thought, I'll go to my brother Eddy and Anne's house; they don't live very far away, just across the big field. And off she went to their house.

That evening Papa came to get her and took her to Grammy's, his mother's house. Honey found out later that he and Esther had a beef. Either he didn't want to take her back, or Esther didn't want her back. That was the first of many trips to Grammy's house.

Whenever she went to Grammy's house, Grammy always took her shopping for new clothing to replace the old-fashioned things she was forced to wear. When Papa brought her back home, Esther always burned all the things Grammy bought for her in the kitchen stove.

There were many residence changes for the family. Esther sold the darling cottage that Papa had built for Mama. The money seemed to go pretty fast. Honey never did know where the money went. She didn't believe her papa did either.

The third move was to a remote farmhouse in the little country town of Bath. She remembers so many things about that place, especially the big barn where Papa had cows and chickens. Every morning he went out to milk the cows and gather the eggs. She remembers the big, wood cook-stove in the kitchen where Esther would burn all her clothes that Grammy bought for her. She remembers the stairway that went up from the kitchen to the upper floor and the big bath room with the great copper bath tub with the big pump that pumped the water into the tub. The tub was all enclosed with pretty cedar wood. Then there was the luscious apple orchard where she could play. And there was a little stream not too far away where Papa would go fishing. Also, there was the big water pump outside where they got their drinking water. It seems the family stayed there about one year.

Then there was the move to a little place in the midtown of Bath, near the tavern where Esther spent most of her time with her friends. They stayed there about six or eight months. That's when Esther gave the orders that Honey was to be called Claire. She didn't want to hear "Honey" anymore. But her papa and brothers still called her Honey.

It seemed that every time Esther and Papa had a fight (this was usually over money) she would take it out on Claire with the strap. Sometimes Papa left Esther and took Honey with him to Grammy's. Grammy loved Papa. Honey can still hear her say, "Ach, my Harry, he's such a good man."

Honey loved Grammy also. She remembers that Grammy couldn't understand why a little girl had to wear boy's underwear and why she didn't have enough clothes. The little girl's daddy wasn't poor. He had a good-paying job, and they seemed to have more than most in those days.

Grammy still called Claire "Honey" too. She would take Honey by the hand and they would both walk a couple of miles down to the general store in Hellertown. Then she would outfit Honey from head to toe with everything she thought she needed. This delighted the little girl.

When they were all through shopping, they went home and Grammy allowed Honey to help her wash the clothes. Honey really liked to do that. She would churn that washer like she was a big lady. Grammy used to say to her, "That's too hard for you to do, you'll be sorry when you get older." But Honey would just keep on pushing and pulling that handle on top of the washer. That was fun for her.

Honey remembers how nice it was when she came home from school for lunch. Grammy would have little cheese sandwiches and fruit and milk all ready for her and served her, just like a queen. Honey never had that at home. She always had to shift for herself.

She really loved living with Grammy.

But it wouldn't last very long. Her papa would come and say, "We're going back home now, Hon." Honey's heart always dropped and Grammy would cry. When Harry and Honey returned home, Esther would be very sarcastic to her and when she saw Honey's new clothes, she would be very irate and immediately take them from Honey and stuff them into the coal stove in the kitchen and burn them. The little girl's heart would break.

Then Esther moved them to a house that was one in a row of houses on Monaccasi Street. Claire remembers when they first moved in. There wasn't a bedroom for her, so she had to sleep on the floor in the room with Esther and Papa. She remembers hearing a lot of heavy breathing from Papa and moaning from Esther all night long. At first, she thought that Papa didn't hear the moaning, as he was very hard of hearing, caused by the war. Then she realized why papa did everything that Esther wanted him to do.

Then the family moved to a farm past Hellertown, which was about fifteen miles out of town. Papa bought a horse to help him plow the fields. That was the only time Honey can remember them having a horse.

Honey remembers this farm very well—it would be on her mind forever. She remembers having to walk five or six miles to a one-room school in the town of Springtown in the snow and rain. All the grades were in the same room.

Other children also walked to school. Papa only had one car, and he had to go about twenty miles or more to the steel mill to work. His work hours changed every week: one week days, one week nights, and one week swing shift. This house was pretty close to Grammy's house, maybe three miles. Honey doesn't remember how long they lived there, but she does remember a Christmas there. Claire was about seven years old. That's when she got the beautiful, brown-haired, brown-eyed doll. The eyes opened and closed, and it was large. Elaine got a blonde, blue-eyed doll, and both received doll carriages. Elaine's was smaller than Honey's. Oh! How Honey loved that doll. This was the first real toy she had gotten since her little furniture was taken away from her. Honey did everything her stepmother wanted her to do so she could play with that doll and carriage.

One day when her papa came home from work, she heard her stepmother and papa talking about a trip to Ohio, which was where Esther and the children were from. As the days went by, there was more talk of the trip. Honey asked her papa if they were all going, and he said, "No."

Then Honey asked, "Am I going?" and he replied. "If you're a good girl, I think you can go."

Honey was very excited and asked, "Can I take my dolly and carriage with me too?"

When Papa asked Esther, she replied, "I suppose you and Elaine may both take them with you." Claire could hardly wait for that day to arrive.

The day of departure came. Esther went into town the day before and brought her sister, Mary, out to the farm. She was joining them on the trip.

Papa came home from work that evening and gave Esther the car to pack up. Papa wasn't going on the trip. He was planning on getting to work by walking quite a long way and catching a streetcar. The distance was five or six miles if he cut across some other farmlands. Then he took the streetcar about ten miles to the steel mill. He was such a sweetheart that he didn't complain of that or of being alone.

It was getting close to departure time. The sun was going down and the evening was becoming dark. It was a nice, warm evening. That was good, as Claire remembers there were six in the car, and the sides of the car were open-air with isinglass shades to hook on if it should rain.

Papa kissed them all goodbye and off they went. Esther was driving and Aunt Mary sat in the front with her. Honey remembers that all the children were excited. The car went down the road about a quarter of a mile and came to an abrupt halt. The children wondered what was wrong. "What's wrong, Mom?' they all asked. Esther got out of the car and said, "Get out Claire." She motioned for Honey to get out.

"What's wrong?" they all asked again.

Esther didn't answer. She went to the back of the car and pulled out the doll with the blonde hair and blue eyes and handed it to Claire and said, "Take this and go on back to your dad."

Claire started crying and said, "Ain't I going with you?"

"No, you go back to your dad," Esther yelled.

Honey refused to take the doll from her, repeatedly saying, "I want my own doll!" She cried. Esther tried to force it on her, but Honey would not take it. Finally, Esther took the doll, stuck it on a tree stump, got back into the car and drove off. Honey started crying, and through her tears she stared at the car driving away. She watched the car, expecting it to stop and go in reverse and pick her up, but it just kept on going down the road. She watched it go out of sight. By then, Honey was crying uncontrollably. She turned around and started back up the hill toward their house. She cried all the way back. Her tears were so heavy she could hardly see the road. By the time she got there it was dark.

She entered the house and there sat her Papa in front of the fire in a rocking chair. The room was pretty dismal since there were no rugs on the floor and very little furniture. Papa seemed slightly surprised, but not too much as she recalls. He pulled Honey up on his lap to console her and told her, "Don't worry, Hon, tomorrow Ralph is coming and will take you to your Aunt Jenny's house in the horse and buggy." Aunt Jenny was papa's sister and lived about twenty-five miles away. Evidently her Papa was planning on having Aunt Jenny take care of Honey since there would be no one at home to be with her when Papa was working.

The next morning, Honey was all excited. She couldn't wait to go for a ride in the buggy. Papa left for work, and Ralph went out and hooked up the horse to the buggy. He called for Honey to come; they were ready to go. So, off they went. What fun that was for Honey. Ralph would make the horse run and the wind would blow her hair. He did things to make her laugh and giggle, and she could wave to all the people they passed.

She doesn't know how far they had gone, but she knows that they were almost there when the horse started slipping on the hard road surface. He tried to keep the horse on the shoulder of the road but couldn't. Then they came to a slight incline and the horse slipped and fell. Ralph got out and helped it up. It could walk, but it limped so badly they had to go back to the farm.

They never did reach Aunt Jenny's. The horse was tied up in the orchard for the night. The next morning Papa would not allow Honey to go outdoors because he said the horse had to be put to sleep. Honey heard the shot and knew the horse was gone. Papa and Ralph buried it in the orchard.

That day was the first time she cooked a full meal by herself. Papa made her a stool for her to reach the sink and the stove. She began making a big vegetable stew for their dinner. Papa said it was delicious. She can remember that like it was yesterday. Once in a while, Papa would show his affection by slipping a quarter or something in her hand as she would pass him in the hall and told her not to let anyone know.

About three weeks later, Esther and her children returned, and it seemed to Honey that Papa greeted them like nothing was wrong. But it was a sad day for Honey because they didn't bring her beautiful doll back to her.

They moved more times, and Honey was taken to Grammy's more times, and her clothing burned more times.

The next move was back to Bethlehem to a house that had more bedrooms. Esther wanted her dad to live with her family as he was in his seventies. He was a very nice man, tall and stately. He was always very nice to Honey and would come to her defense when Esther was mean to her.

Honey remembers the first big console radio that they got when they lived there. One day a man came to the door, selling the beautiful large pieces of furniture that were radios. All the buyer had to do was make a down payment, and he would come back each week for the balance of the payments (if he could catch them at home). This was not unusual, as a lot of merchandise was sold that way. Esther's dad loved to sit and listen to some of the comic programs, like "Amos and Andy." Honey liked to listen to the singers like Kate Smith and Bing Crosby. There was a vacant lot next door to the house and some of the neighbor children would gather there in the evening when Esther was gone and Honey finished her chores. They would sit on the fence and sing all the latest songs like "Blue Moon" and "When the Moon Comes Over the Mountain" and lots of other popular songs.

Finally they moved back to High Street into a tenement house across from the school. Honey was about nine years old. She would sit on the front steps in the evening and watch the children play their school games.

By this time Esther was spending a lot of time with her friends at the taverns. Honey was expected to do the laundry and ironing for the boarders who rented from Esther, and they paid Esther for that. If the house was not cleaned when Esther came home, Honey got punished. Before Esther left, she would say, "It better be done right or you'll get the strap when I come home."

One day, Mr. and Mrs. Schulz, who were neighbors across the field from Claire, came to the house and asked if Claire could come after school and help take care of the new baby they were having, along with the mother. Claire wanted to earn a little money of her own. Finally, reluctantly, she obtained permission from Esther to do this. But it seemed Esther always got the money away from her.

By this time, Claire had become very friendly with one of Esther's nieces—Laverne. They were about the same age. This did not go over well with Esther though. Claire and Laverne got along very well, and when Laverne was permitted to have a party, Claire was invited. Laverne's mother was Esther's sister, Blanche, and she would talk Esther into letting Claire attend Laverne's parties. Claire remembers Laverne would invite boys, and they would play spin the bottle and post office. Since this was about the only fun Claire ever had, she really looked forward to the occasions. Then Laverne's dad suddenly passed away.

Later, Esther decided to move to a bigger house on the corner of Linden and Broadway streets. There Esther could have more boarders. It was a big, three-story home, and Esther was to take in male boarders and Claire was to assist in the cleaning and laundry since she wasn't working for the Schultz's any longer. Claire remembers ironing a lot of men's white shirts.

This went on for about a year. Claire turned twelve years old and became a woman, (a little early). She was in high school with Laverne. Claire remembers that one of her classes was home economics and one was sewing. Claire was pleased with those classes.

Laverne's mother didn't approve of the way Esther treated her stepdaughter. Whenever Claire and Laverne were together, Esther would punish Claire for something. Esther would give orders for Claire to have the house all cleaned after school and "It better be done right," or she would get a beating with the strap.

Laverne would say to Claire, "Why do you stay there? Why doesn't your dad take you away?" and Claire would reply, "He has tried, but she always makes him bring me back to do the work."

"My mom thinks she's terrible to treat you that way," she would say.

Claire would respond, "Someday I'll go away for good." She knew her brothers had tried to take her many times, but Esther would not allow it.

One day Esther and her papa got into another big fight over money again down in the cellar of the house. Claire could hear them going at it. She heard Harry say that he was going to leave and take Honey.

Then he came to Claire and said, "OK Hon, we're going to Grammy's," and off they went. Claire started a high school in Hellertown where Grammy lived. She remembers she wanted to get into the band at the school, but they didn't have an opening for any instrument except the tuba. So Claire said, "That's OK, I'll play that," and she did. She loved music of any kind.

While she lived with Grammy, she met Evelyn, a nice girl with Czechoslovakian parents. They became very good friends. She introduced Claire to a nice boy, and they would double-date and go to the movies.

Evelyn got Claire the job as an upstairs maid for the very wealthy family that she worked for. Evelyn was the down-stairs maid. Claire was happy doing that and having pay coming in. She was happy living at Grammy Diehl's.

That didn't last long though, because her papa took her back home, and Claire had to quit the good job. Esther didn't allow Claire to work for anyone else, as she needed Claire to work for her.

Before Papa agreed to bring Claire back home, he made Esther promise to take Claire over to Allentown and buy her some new clothes, including a new coat. Esther agreed. Grammy Diehl probably told Papa that Claire needed some clothes and a warm coat.

When Claire returned home, they went to Allentown, and Esther did buy her a beautiful coat. Claire remembers it was tweed, kind of brown and gold with a lovely fox-fur collar and cuffs. She loved that coat and felt very grown up in it. She couldn't wait to show it to Laverne.

Soon after that they moved to the same tenement house where they had lived before, across from the school. Things were still the same as before—she still did the cleaning and ironing.

One weekend after Laverne's mother remarried, Laverne asked if Claire could spend the weekend in New Jersey with her. They had a bar and restaurant and an apartment upstairs. She said it would be fun because they could wait on tables and make some tips. Of course, Laverne's mother would be there to chaperone them. Finally, after much persuasion and pressure from her sister, Esther allowed Claire to go.

While Claire was there, she met a nice boy from New Jersey. His name was Bud, and his family had a large farm and was very well known in the area. Claire liked him and his kisses. He was a very mannerly young man and was affectionate with Claire. When Claire went home, he asked her if he could come down to Bethlehem to see her. She said, "Yes," not knowing if her step-mother would allow it, but at that point she didn't care. She liked Bud a lot. So they made arrangements for him to come down the next Sunday. It was the first real date Claire ever had. That was the first time a boy had ever kissed or made love to her. They sat in his roadster and kissed and hugged and talked until it was time for him to leave and drive back to New Jersey.

The next time Laverne went to New Jersey, she wanted Claire to go with her again. Claire had been having such a good time there making tips, and she really wanted to see Bud again.

After much begging and quarreling, she was allowed to go, but she could see that Esther didn't like it at all. This time, Bud took her to meet his family, and they invited her to stay for dinner. They were very nice and seemed compatible with no bickering or arguments, like she always experienced at home. She liked them. They treated Claire pleasantly.

The next day, while Claire and Laverne were working in the restaurant waiting on tables, Laverne came over to Claire and said, "Your stepmother is here and she's telling everyone in the restaurant that you are tied up with Bud and that you're pregnant."

Claire saw red and immediately and went over to the table where Esther was sitting with a group of men. Claire lost her temper and started yelling at Esther, accusing her of harassing her and telling lies about her.

Finally Esther said, "Come upstairs, you little bitch, if you want to yell." Claire could see that Esther was drunk.

So they went upstairs, and Esther's sister followed them. When they got upstairs, Claire said to Esther, "You can't hurt me anymore, no matter how you try. You'll see; you're going to get paid back; you'll be punished for what you're doing to me someday."

Esther's sister agreed with Claire. Little did they know this would come true. Unfortunately, the damage was already done. Claire never saw Bud again after that, and she did like him.

One night when Esther's sister, Mary, had a party at her house, Papa was working, and Esther brought Claire along to babysit the younger children. There was a lot of drinking going on, and some were getting drunk.

They must have gotten low on the booze because Esther came to Claire and ordered her to go with an older guy named Ray. She said, "Claire, you go with him and show him the way back here."

Claire was a little suspicious; she wondered how he got there in the first place. She didn't want to go; she wanted to stay where all the excitement was, but Esther said, "You go!"

Claire didn't know where he was going, but she didn't think it was very far away.

Well, it turned out that he went about five miles away. He stopped the car in front of an apartment house, got out, and came around to her side of the car and said, "Come on in."

Claire said, "No it's OK, I'll wait here."

He said, "No, it is not OK, I don't want to leave you down here. I'll just be a minute."

Claire didn't know what to do. She didn't know this man, and she was afraid, plus it was pretty dark.

He led the way up the stairs to his apartment. He opened the door and motioned her to step in. Inside, Claire just stood there while he went into the other room. She waited to see what he came for. It wasn't more than a couple of minutes and she found out what he came for. He came back out of the other room directly to her and grabbed at her clothes. Then she knew she had to get away from this man. He was pulling her dress up and trying to grab at her panties and pull them off.

Oh my God! She thought, I'll have to tell him I'm in the wrong time of the month.

"Stop," she cried. "You can't do this to me." All this time, she was trying to escape from him by running around and around all the furniture in the room, trying to keep him from reaching her. She finally pulled away and made it to the door. By this time her heart was beating fast. She hoped she wouldn't pass out. She made it out the door and bolted down the stairs two at a time, praying she wouldn't trip and go head first. She reached the outside and kept running. She didn't know where, but she knew the direction of Bethlehem, so she went in that direction.

She ran until she was completely exhausted. It was about one or two o'clock in the morning by then. She didn't know how far she went. Everything became very quiet, so she stopped running and began to walk.

It wasn't very long until she saw car lights approaching from behind her. She got really scared and didn't know where to hide. She was in front of a row of houses, so she had to go back to the beginning of the row to reach the back yards. She jumped over the fence to the first yard in the row. To get out to the street again, she had to climb over the fences of about ten backyards. All the dogs started barking, and she was afraid the owners would come out and see what all the ruckus was about. She didn't know what she would tell them if they did come out.

When she got back on the street, it was empty—no cars—so she began to walk slowly, watching. Soon a car with no lights pulled up beside her and the man said, "Hey kid, come on, get in. I'll take you home."

Claire said, "No, I know what you want."

He replied, "No, come on. I won't hurt you; I can't go back without you. I promise I won't hurt you." After much pleading, Claire finally got into the car. He took her back all the way to Aunt Mary's house without saying a word.

Was he so sure she wouldn't say anything to the others?

Claire knew why Esther insisted on her going with Ray. Esther thought if the guy raped her, she might get pregnant, and that was what Esther wanted. Claire told Laverne and her mother what happened, and they couldn't believe it. As it was, Laverne's mother, and her daughter, Roberta, did not agree with the way Claire was treated. They would tell Esther whenever they had the chance, "Esther, one day you'll be sorry."

Soon after that, Roberta got married and had a baby girl named Robin. One day when Esther and Claire had another big argument, she asked Claire if she would like to come and stay with them and help with the baby. Esther did not like this, but Claire said, "No matter what, I am going." Claire wanted to get away from Esther anyway she could. She liked the offer and Papa agreed. Even though Esther disapproved, Claire packed up her belongings and left. Esther was angry with Blanche, Roberta and Laverne, and she didn't talk to them for a few weeks.

Claire was permitted to go to school, and they paid her seven dollars per week, and she had her own room. Her duties were to do the baby's laundry after school and to dust the house and the spiral staircase before going to school. It was a good arrangement for Claire. Of course she had to change schools again (which was now, several times).

Every chance Esther had, she would do something to start an argument or fight with Claire and harass her. One day, Esther came to Roberta's house and started an argument with Roberta and Claire. She wanted Claire to come back home. It became so intense that they were hitting each other. Soon Esther had Claire down on the floor, punching her. Well, Claire started to punch her back. Esther was about five foot ten and weighed about one hundred and seventy pounds, and Claire was about four foot eight and weighed about one hundred pounds. Finally Esther got up and grabbed Claire's new coat from the closet and ran into the bathroom, which was close by. In a few minutes she came out holding the shredded coat and threw it into Claire's face. She had taken a razorblade and cut it to shreds. Claire almost went into hysterics. Claire loved that coat. Then Claire and Roberta yelled at her to get out and leave them alone.

Things quieted down after a few days, and everything seemed normal for awhile. Claire had met a nice boy at the new high school, and Roberta allowed Claire to invite him to come and see her sometimes in the evening. They would sit in the living room and play records and talk.

It was a Saturday, and Claire was in the basement doing the baby's laundry when Roberta called down, "Claire you're wanted on the phone." Claire couldn't imagine who would be calling her on a Saturday unless it was the boy she had just met. Maybe he was going to ask her out. They were just getting to know each other. She ran up the stairs and grabbed the phone.

The lady on the other end said, "Is this Claire Diehl?"

Claire said, yes, and the lady said, "Well your folks live next door to me, and they wanted me to call you and tell you that your dad had a heart attack, and he's asking for you."

Claire was shocked. She turned to Roberta and asked, "What shall I do? I haven't finished the laundry." Claire was so upset that she didn't have time to ask herself why they didn't call from their own phone. Why did they have a neighbor do it?

Claire didn't know if she could make it there on time. "I'll take the streetcar which has a stop only about four blocks from here, and it will take me to about three blocks from their house, she thought to herself. She practically ran to the streetcar. She didn't think she would ever get there. Finally she reached the house.

It was very quiet as she walked up the front steps and into the entry hall, and she thought, oh God, I hope I got here in time. She walked toward the back of the house where the kitchen was, and there stood her papa washing dishes. Although Elaine was old enough by now to do some of the household chores, he was doing the dishes, and Esther was upstairs lying down, as Claire was to learn later.

At first Papa didn't hear Claire enter. Then she said, "What are you doing? I thought you were sick."

"Who, me? I'm not sick," he said.

"Well, your neighbor called me and said you had a heart attack and I should come right away," she replied.

Before he could answer, she heard another voice from upstairs. "Claire, come up here honey, I want to talk to you."

Claire gave her papa a kiss and started toward the stairs. By this time, she knew it was all a trick, and she was infuriated. As she reached the bedroom, she asked Esther in a very gruff way, "Why did you play such a terrible trick?"

"Because, I needed you to come back here," Esther replied.

"Well I'm perfectly happy where I am," Claire said

"Ok, I'll tell you what I'll do. You know the diamond ring that you always wanted, which belonged to your mother? Well I'll give that to you if you'll come back here and help me with the boarders' ironing and cleaning."

Claire thought for a spell. This is something I've always wanted. If I could just get that ring, I think I could tolerate her for a little while longer, then I'll really get a job and go away, she thought to herself. So she agreed.

Claire related the whole story to Roberta, and she agreed with Claire, but she also thought the trick Esther played was terrible. She understood about the ring and was glad that Claire would finally get it. So Roberta said, "Go, Claire."

When Claire returned to her Papa's house, things seem to go pretty well for awhile. Claire had in her mind to quit school, but she didn't know just when. If this didn't work out she would quit and get a job and leave.

Time went by, and Claire started to wonder when she was going to get the ring. She hadn't seen Esther wear it lately. So, one day she asked Esther, "When can I have the ring?

Esther looked at her, half smiling and kind of sneering. "Oh yes, you can have the ring, but you'll need to go over to Allentown and pick it up."

"What is it doing there? Is it broken or something?"

"No, it's not broken."

"Don't I need a slip or ticket or something to redeem it?"

"No, you just go in and ask for Joe, and tell him what you want. Give him my name, and he'll give it to you."

"Will you take me?"

"No, I can't take you now; I need to go somewhere. You can take the streetcar; it stops right in front of the place. I'll give you the address."

Claire knew Allentown was seven or eight miles away, and it would take a while to get there. So, Claire hurried to catch the streetcar and arrived at the address that Esther had given her. Then she noticed the name on it: Pawn Shop.

She walked in, and a scruffy man greeted her and asked if he could help her. He looked like he was from a foreign country. She told him what she'd come for and gave him Esther's name and described the ring. He went to the case and looked, and came back and said, "I don't have a ring like that."

Claire swallowed hard and said, "But you must, she said she left it here with you."

So he went back to look again. Slowly he came back to Claire and kind of grinned and said to her, "Oh, now I remember, I don't have that ring young lady; that ring was picked up this morning."

The light bulb went on in Claire's head, and she knew that this was another trick. She realized that while she was on the streetcar traveling to Allentown, Esther made a speedy trip over there in the car and picked it up. "Thank you," she said sadly as she walked out the door to catch the streetcar.

As she was riding back to Bethlehem, she was deep in thought about Esther. How can a person be that cruel? She knew then that she had to get away from her, or she would never have a life of her own. She arrived home, but Esther was not there. Claire called Laverne and told her what had happened. Laverne couldn't imagine her aunt doing such a thing, and she called her aunt a "bitch."

When Esther came home, Claire confronted her with her lie and Esther just said, "Well I just changed my mind; I decided I wanted to keep it." Claire just couldn't resist and called her a big liar and a cheat. She accused Esther of knowing all along that she wasn't going to give it to her. With that, Esther gave Claire a hard slap in the face and said, "No one calls me a liar." Claire decided right then that she was going to find a job and get away.

A few days later she saw an ad in the newspaper for help in a millinery shop, so she applied for the job. She decided she would quit school and take the job if they hired her. They did, and she went to work making felt hats. It was quite an interesting job, and she enjoyed the work. Her first paycheck was enough to get her first hair perm.

The day she went to the beauty shop, it was very hot. She wore a dress that Laverne had given to her, a rayon crepe. Claire perspired under the dryer, and the dress shrunk on her, and she could hardly walk. She had to rush home and change her clothes. Laverne always gave Claire her cast-offs, and Claire liked that because they were always good things.

That job didn't last very long as Mr. and Mrs. Schultz, the people she baby-sat for before, called her on the phone and asked her to come to their house; they wanted to talk to her. She made arrangements to go and see them that evening. They were very nice people, and Claire liked them very much; they had always been good to her.

They asked her into the living room to sit down. They explained that they were going to have another child, and they asked Claire to live with them and be a helper. They said they knew what the situation was for Claire at home, and they offered to give her room and board and pay her seven dollars per week. They said she could attend school if she wanted to. That seemed like good pay to Claire. She said she would ask her papa and get back to them the next day.

She went right home and asked him. Esther heard her and said, "Absolutely not! I need her here to help me."

Honey guessed by that time that Papa had seen enough of what was going on, so he said, "Yes, she can; it's close to home, and I'm sure she'll be alright."

By this time, Claire was fourteen—going on thirty. Claire was delighted and she moved in. Claire's room was very nice; she had never had such a nice room of her own. She gathered up her few belongings, the things that she would always keep with her wherever she went. They were a few items of her mother's that she carried with her whenever she changed places to live, so she made sure she had them with her. Some of the items were Mama and Papa's wedding picture, with a few old snapshots of the family, a cut glass bowl in the dot and bow pattern, and a punch bowl with matching glass cups. In fact, Claire still has some of those items. Through all the trials and tribulations, she always carried them with her.

Everything should have gone well now with the new arrangements, but Esther just couldn't stop harassing Claire whenever she had the chance. This was beginning to irritate the Schulz's. Claire tried to think of what to do. She didn't want to go back where Esther lived, ever.

On her times off, Claire would walk up to visit with her brother Eddy and his wife, Anna, and their children. They had four girls, and the oldest was just a little younger than Claire. It was about the only place that Claire could visit, as she had no friends she could count on. She never had an opportunity to keep up a friendship with anyone; Esther made sure of that. Occasionally her friend Evelyn would invite her to double-date with her to a movie.

Finally, Anna said to Claire, "Since Esther is still making things bad for you, why don't you try to locate your mama's sister and your other grandma? I think they're out west someplace, in Arizona or California. You could go see your mama's brother Charley; he lives in Allentown. You could visit him, and he should know where they are; perhaps you could go stay with them out West."

Claire thought this was a good idea, and she decided to pursue it. She checked the phone book for uncle Charley's address and phone number. She called Uncle Charley and made arrangements to see and talk to him and his wife the following Sunday.

When she rang the doorbell, her Uncle Charley came to the door. Claire recognized him from the pictures that Anna had given her of her mama's family. They couldn't get over how she had grown. They hadn't seen her since they were at her mama's funeral. She couldn't remember ever seeing them before. They did have the current address for her mama's sister, Annie, and they thought that Annie's mama stayed with her. The visit was very short as Claire thought the story about her personal situation would be too long to tell them everything.

Claire didn't waste any time writing to her Aunt Annie in California. She didn't think it was wise to ask about coming to stay with them in her first letter. She kept in contact with them for a few months and also tried to save all the money she was earning as pay at the Schultz's. She decided to save all of the seven dollars each week.

So, they corresponded regularly, and Claire tried to learn more about these people. Her aunt told Claire that her grandmother lived in an "old folks" home now, operated by the Church. She found out that they had lived in Arizona at one time and owned and operated a bakery there. During the Depression, they lost all that they had in the banks.

She learned that while they lived in Arizona, they knew an Indian woman who had an illegitimate child and wanted to adopt him out. So, they adopted the baby boy. He would be approximately nineteen years old now.

Finally, Claire described the problems with her stepmother and said at the present time, she was living with and working for other people, but she didn't go into the whole story.

One day, Claire received a letter from her aunt with an invitation to come to them. She immediately showed the letter to Mr. and Mrs. Schultz because she was not yet certain whether she should go or not. They said they understood the decision she had to make and asked her what she thought her papa would say. Claire answered, "Well what can he really say? He isn't caring for me anyway."

Claire couldn't wait to tell Eddy and Anna about the letter. Anna advised Claire to answer and say that she would like very much to come, but right now she didn't have enough money for the fare, so it would be awhile until she could save it. Claire did that right away.

The next letter that Claire received contained a Greyhound bus ticket. Claire was so excited that she ran up to Eddy's house to tell Anna the good news. Anna and Claire talked about it at length and Anna said, "Now you can finally get away from that woman."

"But how can I go? I haven't got a suitcase or things to take. I'll need a warm coat." It was coming into December, and the weather was beginning to get much colder. "Besides, I've only saved up twenty-five dollars."

"Well," Anna said, "you have your ticket, and you'll only need about a dollar a day for food. You can make it. I'll help you get some things together."

And so it was that Claire made her plans to leave. The next payday, she went to town and purchased a nice, heavy coat and began preparing for the trip. Laverne had always given her the discarded clothes she no longer wanted, so Claire had a few things and didn't think she needed anything more. Anna bought her a suitcase and a few personal things—Anna was such a great help to her.

As the day drew nearer, Claire became more excited. She had no idea just how far it was going to be or what kind of a trip it would be. All she knew was that she was going to be away from the harassment of that woman. Everyone was happy for Claire.

A few days before Claire was scheduled to leave, there came a knock on Mrs. Schulz's door. After she answered it, she called up to Claire's room, "Claire can you come down? Your dad wants to see you."

Claire was surprised and happy to see her dad as she didn't see him very often. "Hi, Papa," she said, "What are you doing here? I was going to come and see you soon."

"Will you come out to the car, Hon? I want to talk to you." Claire grabbed her sweater and followed him out to the car. When they got inside the car, he said, "What's this I hear about you going to California?"

"Well, I wrote to Aunt Annie, and they sent me a ticket to come out there," Claire replied."

"I don't want you to go," he said.

"But I want to go, Papa. This is no life for me here. Esther doesn't leave me alone. You must know how she treats me, and you can't seem to do anything about it, so I want to get away from her." By this time, she could see his eyes starting to water.

"You just can't go like that. You're too young, and I can have you brought back."

"How did you find out that I was leaving?" she asked, knowing full well how he knew and also who put him up to stop her from going.

"Esther told me," he said." We can have the police pick you up and bring you back because you're only fifteen years old." She knew Esther had told him.

"Yes, you can Papa, but what would stop me from going again?" she cried.

Then he softened and said, "It looks like you have your mind made up, so I guess I can't stop you. But I want you to remember one thing. If you get out there and you ever need anything you let me know; you remember that." He put his arm around her and hugged her. She knew he meant well, but he would never be allowed to do anything for her without Esther's approval. "Were you going to go without saying good-bye to me?" he asked.

"No, I said I was going to come and see you before I left. You know I don't want to come to that house."

Then his eyes watered more and he put his arms around her and said, "You know I love you, and I know things haven't been easy for you, but I want you to let me know if you ever need anything." With that he kissed her once more, and Claire got out of the car.

Every day after that, Claire expected Esther to send him back, but he didn't come. He must have rebelled at her persistence to stop Claire.

Earlier, Claire had discovered that her youngest brother, Ralph, was working as a bartender at the Republican Club, and she decided to go see him before she left. She didn't know if she would ever be back. She went to see him that night; he was very happy for her. He also informed her that he had met a nice, young lady who he liked very much and was thinking of asking her to marry him. He worked at a little grocery store during the day, and she came in to get groceries. She was Ukrainian. One day, she baked a pie and brought it to him; he must have been smitten. Claire was happy for him. He kissed Claire good-bye and wished her good luck.

# Part Two

CALIFORNIA

Claire's brother Eddy and his family took her to Broadway and High streets, where the Greyhound bus picked up passengers, and they bid her good-bye and good luck. So, with her little luggage and her nice, heavy coat, she climbed aboard for places unknown. Her heart was beating so fast she didn't know if it was fear of the unknown or anxiety and happiness.

As the bus pulled away and started down the road, she looked out the window at all the Christmas decorations and the big lighted star on the mountain behind Lehigh University, as it had been every year since she could remember. The big Moravian church was all lit up, and snow flurries were beginning to fall. This was Christmas, and she was leaving the only home she had ever known. Was she going to miss this little town? She didn't think so, but what could she expect where she was going? She would just have to wait and see. She was finally on a quest for happiness.

The bus driver drove on towards Allentown, and Claire watched the sight of the little town fade away. When they got to Allentown, the driver stopped to let a few more passengers on the bus—it was starting to fill up with more people. Claire felt lucky and safe to get the seat behind the driver. He would talk to her sometimes when something unusual happened on the road.

Soon it became dark, and passengers began to curl up in their seats to sleep. Claire asked the driver if they would be stopping for the night and he said, "No we have to keep on a schedule." Claire was afraid to close her eyes, afraid there would be an accident or something would happen, and she felt she had to be alert, just in case. Exhausted, she wrapped the coat around her and finally dozed off to sleep.

When she awoke, the bus had stopped and people were getting off. It was daylight now "What is it?" she asked the bus driver.

"We're in Youngstown, Ohio, and we're stopping for breakfast and the restroom," he answered.

When they entered the little café, Claire knew she had to watch her spending, so she ordered only a donut and coffee. When she got off her stool and went to pay, the waitress said, "It's already been taken care of,

Miss." Claire didn't know who had paid and was afraid to ask. But Claire did have an idea it must have been the driver. Since she was the youngest on the bus, he may have felt a little protective for her.

The weather began to get much colder, and they drove through more snow. Claire was very glad she had bought the heavy coat because that was all there was to keep warm. They made a stop someplace in Indiana, but Claire couldn't remember the name of it. She looked out of the window of the bus and imagined all sorts of things. What kind of country was she going to? What were the people like? Would she be near Hollywood? Would she ever see a movie star?

Some of the passengers on the bus had musical instruments. One had a banjo, one had a guitar, and one had a harmonica; and pretty soon they all began to play and everyone began to sing. They all agreed that Claire could carry a tune, so they would keep encouraging her to tell them the songs she knew, and they would play them. People were relaxed now that they were acquainted. They all started talking about the next stop—Chicago. Claire had heard a lot about that city but never had a chance to see it. But, it was just another rest stop and a chance to use the restroom.

When they returned and boarded the bus again, Claire felt like she was in limbo; nothing was behind for her, and she didn't know what was ahead. Well, she thought, she would just have to wait and see. Could it be worse than what she left? She was in deep thought as she leaned around the bus driver and looked out the front window. The snow was heavier now, and she watched the tire ruts made in the snow by a truck ahead.

As the bus drove on, the music and singing continued.

Finally, it got dark and the music and singing dwindled away. Everyone seemed to be getting sleepy. The bus pulled up at the curb in front of an old building. It was Davenport, Iowa. Claire leaned over the back of his seat and asked the driver, "Is this a restroom stop?"

"No," he said, "we'll get something to eat here and stay the night because I'm beat, and the rooms are very reasonable."

"Well, I'll just stay on the bus," Claire exclaimed, knowing she probably wouldn't have enough for a hotel room.

"Oh no, you can't do that because they take the bus to clean it out. You must take all your belongings off the bus."

"Well couldn't I just stay in the hotel lobby?" she asked.

The bus driver thought awhile and then said, "What's the matter, young lady, don't you have the money?" he asked.

"Well, I just have enough to get me to California," she answered.

He looked at her with pity and said, "I'll tell you what, I'm going to get a room and you are welcome to share it."

"Oh, I can't do that," she nervously replied. Was this another one of those guys like the one who chased her around the furniture?

Then he said to her, "Well, suit yourself. The offer's open and you won't have to worry about me; I'm too dragged out. We'll both keep our clothes on if that makes you feel better. If I caused you any trouble and my company found out, I'd lose my job. Besides, you must have a place to sleep."

Claire was also very tired. It seemed they had been driving forever. So trusting him; she followed him to the room. The driver disappeared into the bathroom, and Claire didn't know what to make of the situation, but she was so tired. She sat in the chair until he came out, not knowing what his next move would be. He made himself comfortable on one side of the bed. Almost immediately, she could sense he was sound asleep, so she wrapped the heavy coat around herself and stealthily stretched across the foot of the bed. The minute her head hit the mattress she was sound asleep. She never realized he was in the same bed, she was so tired.

When she awoke the next morning, she was the only one in the room. Gosh! Did they all leave her behind? Her heart started to race. Quickly she went down to the lobby. She noticed all the other passengers getting on the bus, but she didn't see the bus driver who had been so kind to her. She asked one of the passengers, "What happened to our bus driver?"

"Oh, this was the end of his run, so we have a new driver and a new bus." Claire felt relieved but sorry she couldn't thank the previous driver for his kindness.

Now, they were off again, and the passengers were back to their music. They talked about getting to a state that wasn't a "dry" state and they could get a bottle of wine. Claire peered out the window of the bus and watched the snow coming down. She wondered if there was going to be more overnight stops. She hoped not.

The weather in Iowa was very cold, and again she was so glad she had that heavy coat. This time, the bus driver furnished some blankets and little pillows. He must have known there was colder weather ahead.

The days seemed all the same, and Claire wondered if they would ever get there and if they would ever get to the warm climate. She was so cold. Claire tried to keep herself amused by looking out the window and seeing things she had never seen before. She saw a lot of desert and mountains without any trees. It certainly wasn't like what she was used to.

The passengers all continued with their music and singing. The driver would point out certain places of interest. She remembers him pointing out Salt Lake City, but she didn't see any lake there.

Finally, everyone on the bus started to cheer. The bus had crossed the line into California. Now they could buy their wine and sing some more, and they did. As the bus drove through San Bernardino and other towns, Claire could see fresh fruit and juice stands and streets all decorated for Christmas. Was she really in California? What was Hollywood like? Would she be able to see that place? What were the people like out here? Who will meet me at the depot? Will it be Aunt Annie? Oh, her heart was pounding now.

Finally, the bus turned and drove down a dirty, trashy street, and Claire could see unshaven disheveled looking men, some sitting on the curb and some sitting against buildings. What kind of place is this, she thought. She had never seen things like this before. Then the bus turned again and pulled up to an old, run-down building and she saw that this was the Greyhound bus stop for Los Angeles. She was told later that the place she had seen was the Skid Row section of Los Angeles where all the drunks and derelicts hung out and begged for anything. Claire had never heard of such a thing before.

As she stepped down from the bus, she looked all around at the people greeting the arrivals to see if anyone could possibly be her Aunt Annie. As she turned to look again, three men approached her and one asked if she was Claire Diehl, Claire said, "Yes, I'm waiting for my aunt to pick me up."

"Oh," the oldest looking one said, "she couldn't come so she sent us to meet you."

"Who are you?" she asked, feeling a little uneasy now.

The oldest looking one explained, "I'm your cousin, Bob, Aunt Annie's son; and this is Mac Hynes, a friend of your aunt and your Uncle Elliot; and this tall guy is Frank. We had to bring him because he's the only one with a car." Then they all started to laugh. They walked Claire to the car and after they stowed her one suitcase in the back, they all piled in.

On the way, the three were competing with each other, trying to win Claire over. She wasn't interested in that right now; she was just interested in seeing her aunt and uncle. As they drove on, her cousin Bob said, "We'll stop at your Aunt Annie's first and then we'll go down to Mac's folks for Christmas dinner. Aunt Annie won't be able to come because she is in bed sick."

After driving about twenty miles, they drove through another little town called Huntington Park. There were a lot of shops along the main street. It seemed to Claire that this would be where everyone would come to shop.

Soon they drove down an old, dirt road and pulled up in front of an old house that probably hadn't been painted for fifty years or more. It was a wood color and had a small porch with a railing that was missing some spokes. They led her inside to the one and only bedroom, where Aunt Annie was lying on the bed.

She was so happy to see Claire that the tears started to roll down her cheeks. Immediately she began to apologize for her condition and the condition of the house. She explained that she had been ill for some time and couldn't get out of bed because her legs and feet would swell up, and then they would have to cut her stockings and shoes off.

Claire said, "Don't worry; you just stay there, and we'll take care of everything."

Claire was in a quandary. She didn't know what to think, but she was here now, and she would need to see her way through it somehow. She began to look around. She had never seen anything like this before. Her folks back home were not wealthy, but she never had to live like this. There were no rugs on the floors, no curtains on the windows, and no paint on the walls. There was a single box springs and mattress on the floor in the small living room. Claire found out later that the Hynes' family donated it to them for Claire. She also found out later that her uncle did not have a job and her cousin Bob was also out of work. They had been living on welfare.

The boys finally brought her back to reality, "Come on, Claire, we must go. The Hynes' family will be waiting dinner for us."

Aunt Annie spoke up and said, "You kids go ahead and have a good time. Mrs. Hynes will send a plate of food back for me." So they were off.

When they arrived at the Hynes' home, things were much different. It was a simple little house, but very neat and clean. The Christmas tree was decorated with packages under it. Mr. and Mrs. Hynes were very sweet, like out of a fairytale. She was short and plump and had beautiful white hair. He was tall and proportionate and also had beautiful, white, curly hair and a white beard. They had two boys, Mac and Julius (who they called Dude), and a daughter named Ruth, who had been married at one time and had a little girl about five years old. They welcomed Claire with open arms. They explained that they would serve dinner first and then open the gifts.

Claire became embarrassed and apologized because she didn't know so she didn't have any gifts for exchanging. Surely they were not going to have gifts for me, she thought. They told her that they did not expect gifts in return.

The dinner was delightful; a real Christmas dinner with all the trimmings—an old-fashion family get-together. Everyone was so congenial. When the dinner was over, everyone headed for the living room, which was so small that they all had to cram in to gather around the tree.

Now it was time to open the gifts. Ruth, the oldest daughter, was to hand them out. They did not forget the new guest—they had gifts for Claire, too. They were not large, overwhelming gifts, but sweet little memento-type things.

The balance of the evening was spent getting more acquainted. Claire learned more about her aunt and uncle—things Claire didn't know before she made the trip. She was reminded that her grandmother was being cared for by the church. Since her grandmother's only relative there was her daughter, Aunt Annie, and she was unable to care for her, the church took on the responsibility.

The evening wore on and all decided it was time to get Claire back to her aunt's house and get into a comfortable bed. She hadn't seen a comfortable bed for the past five days, and she was ready. Since Frank's was the only car available, it was decided that Frank would drive Claire and Bob back to Aunt Annie's place, delivering the food.

Claire prepared her bed on the floor mattress. After bidding good night to her aunt and uncle, she made her way to her bed. She was sure she would fall right to sleep, but she laid there thinking. What was she going to do? Should she look for a job immediately? She wanted to make the house more livable if she was going to be there. But she would need a job to get things the house needed. She began to plan. She wanted to get some fabric and make some curtains for a little more privacy; maybe some rugs to put here and there on the plain wooden floors. And the whole house needed cleaning. The bathroom was out on the back porch, but it did have a bathtub.

Claire thought about some of the places she had lived, and although a lot of them were old, they were never as bad as this. Her papa had always made good money, and they always had plenty to eat. Jobs were always available, but it seemed that everyone was out of work here in this place.

Well, I've got to get something to do to make some money to get these things and to support myself, she thought. Finally she fell asleep.

She woke the next morning to hear her aunt in the next room. The walls were very thin so you could hear almost everything. Her cousin Bob was asleep on a single mattress on the back porch. She could smell coffee brewing and thought they must be having breakfast. She went into the kitchen to check it out. Her Aunt Annie's bedroom was right off the kitchen, and she asked if they all had breakfast.

Aunt Annie answered, "No, I can't get up, and Elliot doesn't cook, and Bob is still in bed on the porch."

Claire went out on the porch and told him, "Get up! Don't you have to go to work?"

"No, I don't have a job," he said.

"Why don't you?"

"There's no work. Sometimes I can get work at the wrecking yard."

With that she said, "Well you better find something; you can't go on like this forever. I guess I'll have to find a way to make some money." She walked into the kitchen to make breakfast.

Aunt Annie said they had some ducks in the back yard, and when she could get up, she would use the duck eggs for breakfast. So, Claire made pancakes with the duck eggs. This was a first for her, as she had never cooked with duck eggs before.

After they all had breakfast and she cleaned up the kitchen, Claire decided to walk around the neighborhood and see what was available. She met a lady who lived in the next house, and they began to talk about her aunt and uncle. She brought Claire up to date on some of the things Claire wanted to know. The lady lived in a house just like Aunt Annie's, and they seemed to be very poor also. She was getting help from the Salvation Army. She and her husband had four children, and every morning she'd get out the mop and bucket and mop her wooden floors until you could almost eat off them.

As Claire walked on, she approached the corner of the main street and noticed an antique store. She looked through the window at all the pretty crystal and glassware. Suddenly she had an idea. She would ask the man if he would buy her punch bowl. That would get her some cash. So she went in and explained to him that it was her mother's and asked if she could bring it in for him to see what he would give her for it. He said, yes, but he had several in stock at that time and he couldn't promise her much.

The next day, Claire took the set to him, and he looked at it. He said, "I'll tell you what I'll do for you. Since this was your mother's, I'll loan you fifty dollars, and you can come back and redeem it any time. That was a lot of money then, so Claire accepted the offer. Now she could make the curtains for the house. And that is what she did.

A few days later, some people from the church where her grandma was staying came to the house. They had heard Claire was there, and they wanted to hire her to take care of a family from the church who were all ill with the flu. Since Claire just came from the cold climate, she had built up a resistance. They would pay her, and she could come home every night. Claire went to work for them for a couple of weeks.

Claire finally became irritated with Bob for not working. Every night he would come home with the smell of beer on his breath. One night she told him that if he came home smelling like he had been drinking all day, she would sober him up real quick. When Aunt Annie heard that she said, "You do that Claire."

The next night when Claire got home, there was Bob on his bed, and she could smell the beer when she entered the porch. "OK, now I warned you. You're going to straighten up and go find yourself a job and no more drinking beer all day."

Then she went into the bathroom and turned the cold water on in the tub to let it fill. She grabbed him by the arm and pulled him off the bed. She didn't know if she could do this or not. He was six feet tall and about one hundred and sixty pounds, and she was five feet tall and about one hundred and fifteen pounds. She was going to try. He didn't resist. However, as she directed him toward the bathroom and he saw the tub of cold water, he must have known what was coming. He started to plead with her.

"Oh, Claire! No! Don't. Don't do this to me!" he pleaded. She got him in the tub of cold water, clothes and all. Then he promised he would straighten up and get some work and not drink beer all day. She knew the only reason she conquered him was because he didn't want to hurt her—he was a big, husky guy.

His friend, Frank Lehning, was coming around calling on Claire quite regularly. So it was that all three boys were on the make for Claire, even her adopted cousin Bob. On the weekends when Frank wasn't working, all of them would go out together. Usually it was down to the beach at a place called Lick Pier for dancing and a few drinks. Frank was the only one who had a steady job. So they all piled into Frank's car, and the boys would stock up on beer and other drinks. They always got sloe gin for Claire because she hadn't done much drinking. They all had a great time. This went on with first Frank calling on Claire, and then it was Mac Hynes coming to call. And because Bob didn't have a car, he always went along with the rest of them. They were all trying to propose to Claire, and it was becoming a comedy. Aunt Annie was getting a real kick out of it.

This went on for about three months, during which time Claire fixed up the house and got a job at the Diamond nut factory shelling and sorting nuts. It paid a set amount for a burlap bag of premium nuts. She had to ride the streetcar way downtown, but it was a job.

One day, the church informed Claire that they had to bring her grandma to the house. Claire would have to take care of her, as they could not handle her anymore. So Claire made herself a bed on the floor and gave grandma her bed. Grandma slept all day and ranted and raved all night. Claire worked all day, but she didn't get much sleep at night. She had been in California about two and half months by this time.

Nearly two weeks later, Grandma went out of her head, and no one could handle her. Aunt Annie said, "We better call the paramedics." So Claire called them, and they came out and took her to the hospital. She was only in the hospital a couple of days before she passed away. Claire had to make all the burial arrangements as her aunt was unable to get out.

In the meantime, Frank was becoming more insistent about marriage. Claire thought about it a lot and talked to her aunt. Frank was a nice boy, and very mannerly. He had a steady job, and it would get her out of this situation. Maybe she wouldn't have to work in the factory. She decided to accept his proposal. She was sixteen now and, she thought, I might as well be married. Even though she had no deep love for Frank, she did like him a lot.

They were married in a little chapel in Hollywood. It was difficult to find apartments to rent, but they found a place in what people call a court—small, attached cottages around a central court. It was a studio—one room used as both a living room and a bedroom, plus a bar kitchenette and a bathroom.

Frank wanted Claire to quit her job, which she did. She stayed home and had dinner ready for Frank when he returned from work, which is what he wanted. A few weeks later, Claire got word that her aunt had passed away. Claire had to make all the burial arrangements again. So within six months after arriving in California, she lost her grandmother and her aunt and had no blood relatives left at all.

The boys and Frank kept up their comradeship, and they all still went dancing.

Then one day when Frank came home from work, Claire said she had something exciting to tell him. She didn't tell him right off, and he kept asking her, "What is it?" Finally she told him they were going to have a baby. He was delighted.

Claire was beside herself with joy. She had dreamt about having her own baby. She decided she would write to her dad and tell him. She received a letter back, saying they were real happy for her and that Claire should come home so they could take care of her. Claire wasn't very happy about that. She was getting along fine.

Finally after a few more persistent letters, Frank said, "Why don't you go?" By this time, Claire was about five months along and she felt good. She didn't think the trip would do her or the baby any harm. After all, Esther said everything would be alright taking the bus. Claire couldn't afford a doctor, so she was just going by people's advice. So off she went, anxious to show everyone how happy she was to have her own little bundle of joy.

After another five-day trip, she arrived home. It was a tiresome trip, but she was happy. She was expecting her own baby. After two days, she began to feel very uncomfortable and started passing blood. She immediately became alarmed and told Esther who informed her that it was nothing to worry about. But it became worse. Soon Claire was writhing in pain. They called the ambulance, and she was taken to the hospital where she was immediately sedated.

When she woke up, the nurse told her she had lost the baby—it had been a boy. Of course, Claire was very upset and inwardly blamed Esther for giving her bad advice. She thought that Esther should have known the trip would not be good for her. Esther and her dad notified Frank, and he came as soon as he could. As soon as Claire felt well enough, she and Frank headed back to California.

Claire became restless. She was thinking of going back to work. She didn't know what that would be, but she was going to look. Frank went back to his job, but things were not the same between them. Before the miscarriage, he always came from work at the regular time. Now, he was not coming home, and Claire would be upset wondering where he was. Things went on like that for awhile and one day Claire decided to get in the car and go look for him. She found him with the boys sitting on a curb, drinking. That was enough. She asked him what he thought he was doing. He said, he was doing what he wanted to do and told her to go home. When he returned, she told him she wouldn't put up with his behavior and if he wanted it that way, then she would leave him. He said that was the way he wanted it. So he went back to live with his folks.

Claire talked to her friends, the Hynes, and they offered her a place to stay with them. She could sleep with Ruth and her daughter, and maybe Mac could get her a job at General Controls where he and Ruth worked. Claire went to see his boss and got a job with that company.

Things were going along good for Claire, and she was happier now that she had a good job. She had made lots of friends, and they would all go out after work and have fun. In the meantime, Claire was thinking of getting a divorce, but Frank would not agree. He decided that he would enlist in the Army. Claire's cousin Bob signed up in the Marine Corps at the same time. There was a lot of talk about war, and jobs were becoming more plentiful.

One night, the group from work went to a little bar at the small, local airport to have fun before going home. The place was called The Cockpit and was a replica of a real cockpit from a plane. The owner and bar tender was "Doc Dinky." They nicknamed him "Doc" because a lot of the servicemen would come in and sometimes they had a little too much to drink, resulting in a hangover the next day. Then they would come to him for a remedy. He was adorable. He was a small, good-looking man, just about Claire's size. They started playing music, and Claire started singing. Well it wasn't long before they all had her up on the bar singing.

That was the beginning of a beautiful friendship. Doc started calling Claire "Judy" because he thought she looked like Judy Garland, and she could sing like her. This went on night after night. Doc was stealing Claire's heart. The rest of the group called the two of them a pair, and wherever Claire was, so was Doc.

One night he said to her, "If you can wait 'til I close tonight, I'd like to take you somewhere." So, Claire made arrangements to do that. He took her to a place in a hotel where they had a broadcasting station and made recordings. He had Claire sing some songs, and he made recordings of her singing. When they were all finished, Claire said she had better head for home, as it was after midnight and it took about an hour to get home. There were no freeways at that time.

Doc said, "No way are you going to drive that far at this time of night. You can stay with me and go to work from my place." By that time, Claire was pretty tired and took him up on his offer. When they were at his place, he became more amorous than usual, but Claire was ready for that since she liked him very much.

Claire stayed many nights with him. He was wonderful to her. He would give her his shirts to wear since they were the same size, and he would say she looked cute in them.

Claire had been working at General Controls for about six months when one day her boss called five or six of the workers aside, including Claire. He said he was going to work for a place called Air Research, which manufactured airplane parts and controls, and he wanted to take them with him. The pay would be much better and it would be closer to their homes. He said that if they would like to go, they should let him know. Of course they all, including Claire, accepted.

Claire liked her job at the new factory. First she was in the engineering department working on blueprints, then because the company became really busy, she was transferred to the drill press line. Claire was very happy about the pay increase, but she didn't get to see Doc as often as she wanted—she was too far away. She was real sad about that. He came to visit a couple times, but it was too far for him to be away from his business at those late hours.

Claire made some new girlfriends and started going out with them and having a ball. They would go to the military dances. Sometimes they would go to San Diego to the naval base where she met a nice sailor from Georgia. She would meet him every time they went down there. One time, he took her for an airplane ride. It was the first time in a plane for Claire. He wanted her to marry him, but he was shipped out before their romance went any further.

They always went as a group of girls and had lots of fun. One of the girls had a  boyfriend who drove a motorcycle. Her name was Marjorie, and she had a complete motorcycle outfit. She introduced Claire to a guy with a motorcycle and encouraged Claire to get an outfit too. So every weekend, off they would go riding, making rounds of all the cycle bars and having fun.

When the two Hynes' boys got married to girls from their church, Ma and Pa Hynes gave their little shack to Claire to live in. She didn't see Doc much anymore as she was busy working and had made other acquaintances.

To make extra money, she took a side job at a little donut shop nearby, working nights for a few hours. Next to the donut shop was a bowling alley. Claire took up bowling and became acquainted with the people who owned it. They had a daughter, Dora Mae, and she and Claire would bowl there free when they had a chance. Dora Mae was still going to school. She was a wild one.

One day, Dora Mae's dad told Claire he was going to open a duckpin alley next to the bowling alley and asked if she would like to run it for him. It would only be open in the evening. That sounded good to Claire as she was still working at Air Research.

So it was that Claire went to work for Mr. and Mrs. Van Horn. They had a nephew named Richard who drank a lot. He would come around the bowling alley quite often when Claire was still in the donut shop. He always wanted to take Claire out on a date. The Van Horns liked him to associate with Claire because she wouldn't let him drink. They went out several times and spent a lot of time together in the duckpin alley. Being around him so much, Claire began to call Mr. and Mrs. Van Horn Aunt Dorothy and Uncle Bert, and they became very close friends.

One evening when Claire was behind the desk at the duckpin alley, the intercom phone from the bowling alley rang, and Claire answered it. "Hello, how are you doing over there?" came the man's voice.

Claire answered, "Fine, and who is this?"

"This is Albert, the manager of the other side."

"Oh, I'm doing great."

He said, "It's kind of slow over here tonight. Why don't you come over? I'd like to meet you."

Claire responded, "Well I have a couple of lanes going right now. I'll come over when I close up."

When she closed up, she went over and met Albert. He seemed like a real nice man, very neatly dressed and nice looking, probably five or six years older than Claire. She noticed he had a limp, but it didn't seem to bother him at all. He said he bowled a lot and at one time bowled three-hundred, which as far as Claire knew, was really good. He told her he was from Illinois and came to California with some other guys. This was the only work he knew as it was what he did in Illinois.

Albert visited Claire in her alley often, and then one night he asked her if he could take her out for a drive and maybe something to eat. Claire accepted. They went for a drive the next night and as it was getting late, he said, "I wanted to buy you dinner but I'm short of money until I get paid."

"That's alright," Claire said, "I have money; where shall we go?" They decided on a drive-in restaurant.

After that, every night Albert was on the phone calling the duckpin alley. There were many nights he wanted to go out, but it seemed most of the time he didn't have money, but Claire had money because she had two jobs, and one was a good paying job.

Things became a little serious as far as Albert was concerned, and it wasn't long until Claire noticed that Albert would be upset when he learned she had been out with someone else. Claire liked Albert, but other men wanted to take her out, and she wanted to go. One was the Van Horn's nephew. And then there was the group at Air Research that had parties and picnics, and Claire loved to go. Claire loved fun and liked a good time.

Albert became more and more attentive, wanting to see Claire every night. He would bring her flowers or a corsage whenever he came to pick her up. Sometimes they would have an argument and he would leave with a pout, but the next night he would come with flowers to make up. One night they had an argument about getting married. They were in that little shack that the Hynes' let her live in. It was a very foggy night.

Albert said to her, "See that fog out there? I'm going to drive into it, and I don't care where I end up." With that he took off, angry.

He became more adamant about getting married, and Claire didn't know what to do. She talked to Ma Hynes and Ruth, her daughter, and they both advised her not to marry him. They said, "It won't work out for you Claire. He is too sensitive, and you will be unhappy." Claire didn't know what to do. She wanted a life with someone who really cared about her, and she wanted children. People were restless with the war coming closer.

Finally she told Albert she would marry him, but he would need to wait until she had her divorce. He didn't want to wait. He said, "You know my aunt lives in Las Vegas. I'll talk to her and ask if you can stay with her while you get the divorce."

That sounded all right to Claire, but she said, "What about my job?"

He replied, "I don't want you to work anyway, so you can quit your job."

Claire hated to leave that good job at Air Research, but he insisted. So she quit her job at both Air Research and the duckpin alley. It was the biggest mistake she ever made.

Claire took off for Las Vegas to stay with Albert's Aunt Martha who turned out to be a fun person. Claire got along very well with her. Aunt Martha's place wasn't big enough to accommodate more than one person. It was one room and bath—and one bed, but Claire managed to bunk in with her.

Claire applied for the divorce and had to wait a short time for it to be final. In the meantime, Aunt Martha got Claire a job in a restaurant there where she made good tips, and people seemed to like her. The gamblers would come in for a cup of coffee on their breaks and after paying five or ten cents for the coffee, flip her a silver dollar as a tip.

Albert's aunt did not think Claire should marry Albert either. She would say, "He's too jealous. He wants you under his thumb." She tried to get Claire together with the guys she knew—Claire thought Albert knew that because one day, here comes Albert. She had not expected him and was surprised to see him. Claire decided that he came to check on her. He would keep himself busy gambling and come into the restaurant where Claire worked and hint for money. Claire would give her tips to him so he would leave her alone. But he soon had to return to California to his job.

Before the divorce was final, Claire received word that Frank had drowned in the Colorado River while on maneuvers for the Army. The attorney found out by notifying the Army about the divorce. Therefore

Claire didn't need to go through with the divorce, and she returned to California.

She was notified by the Army that Frank had money coming, and it should go to Claire or his parents. At that time, there was no insurance money from the Army. Claire decided the money should go to his parents as she thought they needed it more than she did.

When she returned to California, she and Albert made plans to marry. They started to look for a place to live. It was very difficult to find a place because of the coming war. Also as soon as Albert's folks—who lived in Illinois—heard he was getting married, they decided they would move to California and be there for the wedding.

Claire and Albert had a nice, quiet wedding in a little chapel in Huntington Park. Pa Hynes gave Claire away. One of their boys was best man, and one of the boys' wives was maid of honor.

Now they had to find a place to live, as well as a place for Albert's folks. His mother wanted to come to California to get his dad away from his drinking buddies—they were all big drinkers.

Claire and Al found a place they could afford in a transformed, one-room garage with a bath. Claire found another place for his folks. One day, his mother came over and said she found a place for Claire and Al near them, on her way from church. It was nice, and she thought they could afford it.

Claire and Al went right over to see it and loved it. It was a small, two-bedroom house with two other houses on the lot, and it was all fenced in. The landlady lived in the front house. As soon as they could, they moved in. They hoped they would be able to afford it, since Claire wasn't working now.

Claire began immediately to improve the interior. Furnishings and appliances were very difficult to buy due to the war. Claire found draperies made of paper and installed them. She also saw an ad in the newspaper that a man wanted to sell a complete house full of furnishings. Claire went to see what he had and how much he wanted for all of it. He had an old high-oven-type stove and he wanted one hundred and fifty dollars for everything. She decided to buy everything and try to sell the things she didn't need. She sold all the other things and ended up getting the things she needed for nothing. So, little by little, she made it very comfortable. But it was getting difficult to make ends meet with the small wages Al was making at the bowling alley, and he was having a problem with the men he was working with. Claire encouraged him to look for another job, but he didn't seem to have the push.

One day after a money argument, Claire said to him, "You know Al, you've had a good education, going to business college, and you're smart at figures. You should be able to find something along that line."

Jobs were plentiful then due to the war. One night, he came home and told Claire that he had an argument with the man at work and quit. Claire said, "Oh good, now you can look for something better."

One of Claire's friend's husband was working at a factory that was making war products and said that they were hiring. Claire told Al that he should go and check it out. He did and got a position in the personnel department. Claire was delighted. But Al didn't think he could handle it.

Claire said, "Yes, you can; you're good at figures." So he took the job.

Al had three sisters who lived in Peoria, Illinois, where his folks were living before they came to California. Two of the sisters decided to come to California too. The third sister decided to stay in Illinois, as she was presently having a problem with her husband. He was a minister of the Mennonite Church there. She met him when she played the organ and piano for the choir. They had a son, and he was about six years old at the time.

Soon after Claire and Al had rented the little house, the landlady decided they were going to move to Oregon and her house would be for rent. Al told his parents, and they decided they wanted to rent it so they would be closer to Claire and Al

For Claire and Al, things were getting pretty slim financially, so Claire told Al she'd like to go back to work. He wasn't very agreeable, but it was becoming harder to make ends meet. And they were not getting along very well.

One day after Al left for work, Claire dressed up and took the street car to the factory where Al worked and applied for a job. The manager who Claire spoke to left for a few minutes during her interview and came back and said, "You're hired."

Claire discovered later that he went in to Al and said, "There is a young lady out here who wants a job. Her name is Claire. Should we hire her?"

Al said, "Yes, I guess if she wants to work, let her have it."

So Claire went to work riveting ailerons (part of the wing) to airplanes. Claire worked there for about a year. She was very happy to be bringing in more money to help with the finances. The bosses seemed to like Claire and thought she was a good worker.

One day, her boss came over to her while she was riveting and motioned for her to follow him. After they walked over to another department he said to her, "Do you see that space that's marked off?"

Claire looked and replied, "Yes."

"Well I want you to stand in the middle of it and I'll send Gus, the maintenance man, over, and you tell him what you want for a tool check-out station. You'll be in charge of all the tools checked out by workers." Claire was off the riveting line. She received a raise in pay and had that job quite a while

One day, after feeling sick for a few days, Claire came to the conclusion that she was pregnant. She visited the doctor, and he confirmed her suspicions. She really wasn't ready for motherhood, and the thought of having her own baby overwhelmed her. As she began to feel better, she decided to stay on the job a little longer. That way they would be able to better afford the baby. Al didn't want her to work, but she thought six months would not be difficult.

So in six months she gave up her job and prepared for the baby. She crocheted little things and made a pretty bassinette in preparation. She didn't know if it would be a boy or girl. Whatever it would be, she wanted pretty things for her baby.

Things were becoming a little rocky between Claire and Al because of his jealousy and his harassment on small issues like buying something he didn't approve of, or being friendly with someone he didn't approve of. He would regularly ridicule Claire in the presence of other people. He seemed to enjoy putting her down.

One evening while his sister and her male friend were visiting, and they were all playing cards, Claire made a play that Al thought was incorrect. So he laid into her, and told her how stupid she was. She was so embarrassed by his remarks, she started crying. His sister and her boy-friend were so embarrassed that they got up from the table and went outside for a walk.

Claire thought to herself then that if she wasn't pregnant with this child, she would walk out. Instead she became more and more anxious for her baby. She hoped it would be her companion, that she would have someone close to her.

It was nearly Christmas and Claire, as usual, had everything ready for the holidays, just in case the baby came. Well, five days after Christmas, she began to have labor pains, and she knew the baby decided it was time. Claire was rushed to the hospital and after several hours of horrific pain, at 11:42 a.m., the beautiful boy was born, weighing a great eight pounds and five and three-quarter ounces. Little baby Alan was laid in Claire's arms.

What a joy that was! Claire took great care of her precious ward. She really enjoyed the closeness when she nursed him. When she took him to the grocery store in his stroller, allowing the passing people to stop and admire the pretty baby, Claire would glow with pride.

Things between Claire and Al were still the same, and finances were the main issue.

Al's dad was still drinking a lot, and one night on his way home, crossing the street, he was hit by a motorist. He was disabled for several months.

Al's parents couldn't manage the cost of medication, so Al and Claire took on the responsibility.

One day she decided that it would be nice to take a trip back to Pennsylvania and see her dad and show him their beautiful son. Al agreed and decided to drive there.

When they arrived, her papa was very happy to see her and loved and cuddled his grandson. Esther's daughter, Elaine, was there. Claire always liked her. She noticed that Elaine was pregnant, and there was no husband around. She finally learned that she had been at a saloon with her mother one night, and Esther encouraged her to go with this guy (who turned out to be married) to take her home. Well, he raped her, and this was the result. Claire felt so sorry for Elaine. She was a timid girl. At the time, Claire thought to herself, well Esther, many people told you that you would pay for the treatment you gave me and I guess this is it. The only problem is that it was Elaine who paid.

Claire and Al did not stay very long, as Esther would make sarcastic remarks to them, and they didn't feel welcome. They decided to go to Illinois and visit Al's sister, Della.

When they arrived, Della was so happy to see them and the baby. They noticed her husband, Frank, was not around. "Where's Frank?' they asked.

She answered, "Well, he's not here now, but he stays out in the garage. He has a bedroom out there."

"Wow, what's up?"Claire asked.

Della and Claire sat up until way past midnight chatting. Frank had become very active with the young people in the church, taking his authority too far. At the young people's social gatherings and camp-outs, he took up with a young girl and got her pregnant. Can you imagine that, a minister of a church!! He asked Della for a divorce, and she refused, quoting the Bible.

As they sat there discussing the situation, Claire said to her, "Della, I know you feel cheated and discarded, and I know you are very religious and live by the Bible, but this man has betrayed the marriage trust and wants to be free, and you are forcing him into a position he can never fulfill. Doesn't it say something in the Bible about being a millstone around someone's neck? I'm not as religious as you, but I do think being a millstone is also a sin. Give up, Della, and he'll pay later, and you will be happier for it. You can always come to California and stay with us until you get straightened out."

While they were there, little Alan would play with Della's son, Frankie, in the front yard, and Claire would check on them every few minutes to see if they were OK. One time, when she went out, she didn't see Alan, and Frankie didn't know where he was. Della had mentioned that there was a train track at the end of her street. A limited train called the Bullet would fly down that track from Chicago. They didn't see how Alan would get out of the yard as it was gated and had a high hedge surrounding it. Nevertheless, Claire became upset and went out to look for him. As they walked up the street, they saw a man carrying little Alan. Claire was beside herself thinking Alan might be hurt. The man said, "No, he's OK. I saw this little guy up by the track playing and didn't know who he belonged to, so I picked him up. I was trying to find who he belonged to." Needless to say, Claire was very relieved. Alan had crawled through a small opening in the hedge and decided to go exploring.

On the drive back to California, Claire and Al hit snow when they got to Colorado. The car got stuck in the snow, and Al had a hard time getting it out. He noticed a fence post, holding a fence, so he yanked it out and put it under the wheel and got the car free to drive on.

A month after returning home, Claire received a letter from Della saying she divorced Frank and she was coming to California. Claire was happy to hear that. Della came and stayed with them and found a job right away in a candy factory making chocolate. She had experience doing that, in Illinois. She also joined a church close by and became the organ player for the choir.

It wasn't long before a man in the congregation noticed her and was smitten. One Sunday he asked if he could take her out. She came home and asked Claire, "What should I do?"

Claire said, "Go, of course. You only have yourself to answer to." That was the beginning of a beautiful romance. It wasn't too long before they got married. Claire and Della were to remain friends from that time on.

In the meantime, Claire decided she would need to go back to work. The baby was almost two years old now. One of her friends worked at a furniture factory sewing upholstery, and she mentioned to Claire one day that her boss was looking for seamstresses. Claire said she had never done that. Her friend, Grace, said, "You can sew on a sewing machine can't you?"

And Claire replied, "Sure."

Grace said, "Then you can do it."

Claire talked to Al's mother to see if she would agree to watch the baby so she could take the job. She was delighted because she loved her little grandson. Besides, it would repay Claire and Al for helping them with the medicine—also, Claire agreed to pay her a fair amount to do this.

So Claire went to work for the furniture factory sewing sofa skirts and cushion covers. The bosses said she was doing well and did very neat work. Most of the workers were from Mexico and not very educated. Some could hardly speak English.

She worked there about three or four months when one morning while Claire was sewing away, one of the bosses came over to her and said," I think you're the best one here for this job. Do you think you could take inventory of rolls of fabric and keep a log of it?"

Claire replied, "Well I ran a tool crib once and kept track of all the tools." So Claire was in charge of all the fabrics. She also received a raise in wages.

Within several months, Claire was promoted to an accountant assistant with another pay raise. The owners were very good to Claire; they would do nice things for her. When they went on a trip or vacation with their wives, they would always bring something back for Claire. On occasions when Al didn't pick her up after work, they insisted on taking her home. They didn't like the idea of her taking the streetcar that far. Al would become very jealous about the attention, and that would stir up more trouble at home for Claire.

Very late one night, while Claire was sleeping, she heard a noise she thought came from the baby's room. She jumped out of bed and went in to check if the baby was alright. When she looked in the crib there was no Alan. She became alarmed and thought immediately that someone came in and kidnapped her baby. She looked all over the house and didn't see him. She called to Al to help her. They both went outside and looked down the street but no Alan. So she decided to call the police. When she walked into Al's parent's house to use the phone, she went into their bedroom first to tell them and low and behold, there was Alan in bed with them. What a surprise that was! He had climbed out of his crib and out the back door into his grandma's house into her bedroom.

Claire must have worked at the fabric factory for about two years when she realized that she was pregnant again. She wasn't very happy about that, as the situation between Claire and Al was so unpleasant. Claire tried to stay away from sex with him. She would wait until he got to bed and asleep before she went to bed so he wouldn't bother her, but that didn't always work. Claire decided she would need to make the best of things since she was going to have two children to care for now. She decided she would work until it was time for the baby. Again, the two men she worked for were very good to her. They bought the baby's crib and other things for her and the baby. Of course, that made Al upset and jealous, and there was always an argument. She worked until the day before the baby came. Jerry was another beautiful boy and a very good baby.

After the baby came, Claire had to find work. So she decided to proceed with her decorating knowledge. Al's parents cared for Alan, the older child, but Claire took Jerry with her to meet with the clients. She put the baby's car bed in the car and took him all over with her. She would obtain the clients through her connections with the furniture company she had worked for, and the arrangement seemed to work well for everyone.

Meanwhile, renting was becoming difficult. Landlords were raising rents and evicting tenants so they could raise the rent. They were making all sorts of deals. The government made it possible for landlords to take their rentals away from tenants by saying they or their families needed the place to live.

So Claire and Al's landlady said they were coming back to California and needed her house for her sister. She also said she needed the house in front where Al's parents lived. Al's parents found a rental nearby, but Claire and Al didn't know what they would do. They couldn't find a rental, and they didn't have money for a down payment on a new house.

By this time, Claire was working on her own as an interior designer, and she was doing well, making good money. But things between Al and Claire were not getting any better. He became more argumentative and found fault with everything she did. And he was more suspicious about everything. He would do spiteful things, and then later he would bring flowers or a gift so she would forgive what he did or said. It seemed as though the refrigerator was always full of gardenias. It was a complete hassle, and Claire felt that she just couldn't take this much longer. Claire thought if they could only find another place to live it might ease things up a little.

One day as Claire was driving around looking for a house, she spotted a new home on a corner near a railroad. The price was not too high, but she still would need a small down payment. It was a very nice two-bedroom home.

If I could only get the down payment, thought Claire. She decided she would try to borrow the money. It was only fifteen hundred dollars, and she knew that as long as she was making money doing interior decorating, she would be able to repay a loan. So she borrowed the money and purchased the house.

They moved in, and Claire did a decorating job on it. She got a lot of the furnishings from the furniture factory where she had worked. That made Al jealous. Things were still not very compatible on the home front—arguments all the time. And because Claire was on the road working, Al became jealous and argued about everything Claire did. If she came home late, he would accuse her of being with other men. If she purchased something he didn't approve of, or if she wouldn't do things his way, it was an argument. There always seemed to be a hassle, and it stressed Claire.

By this time, Al had quit his job as personnel clerk at the factory and took another office clerk job for Pratt-Whitney Co. One day they had a big argument. Claire told Al that she was going to leave as she couldn't stand the hassling and arguing any longer. This was in the morning before he took Alan over to his parents who were to watch him that day.

When Claire returned home that evening, Al was there, but no Alan. Claire asked him "Where's Alan?"

Al responded, "Well, I'm not bringing him back, and if you're leaving, you're not taking him." That really started a big row.

One evening, with Alan still gone, Al came home and showed Claire a rope. He said, "See this? I'm going in the garage and use it, and maybe it will end all this."

Claire thought, how can I bring these boys up in this kind of household? I've got to do something. I can't stand this much longer. The next morning Claire packed up the baby and some of her things and left the house. She decided she was really going to make a big change, somehow. She would see an attorney and make Al bring back her other boy. Then she would find another place to live where she wouldn't need to go through this anymore.

She decided she would try to find another place to live first. She didn't care about the house—she would leave it. If you can't be happy, it's not your home, she thought. She did find a place, and the landlady agreed to take care of the baby while Claire worked. To Claire it seemed like a good arrangement. All she needed to do now was get an attorney to get her other boy back.

In a week, Al discovered where she lived and he came to talk to her. He had Alan with him and she got to see him. He wanted to make a date the next day to take her to lunch and talk over the problem, and she agreed. He came the next day, without Alan, and they went to lunch. After discussing it, Claire agreed, for the children's sake, to return to the house and give it a try. She didn't want the boys separated.

They both decided to sell the house and find a place further out in the country where they thought it would be better for the boys. It was a little difficult to sell the house because of the railroad being so close. Claire thought they should get what they put into it, and Al thought they should make more on the sale. Claire said, "We have only put in a new water heater, and we lived here three years. The payments were just like rent and if we can get out of it what we put into it, I think we are lucky." (Well it so happened they did.)

While they were out looking for a place in the country, they found a half-acre lot in a walnut orchard that was for sale. The two men who owned it were contractors. Claire and Al really liked it. Now all they needed to do was sell their place and try to get the money to buy this.

In the meantime, Claire knew the daughter-in-law of the owner of an appliance store where she was buying merchandise for her decorating jobs. Her name was Barbara Marshall. One day, they came up with the idea of opening a shop of their own where they could sell things at a discount, and Claire could do the decorating for a fee. Claire was able to get the furniture they would need for the shop from her friends at the manufacturing company where she had worked. Barbara found an empty store on Sunset Boulevard in Los Angeles with reasonable rent. So they started another venture. They named the shop "Claire and Barbara's."

While they were working there, Claire met a policeman who was on the beat, checking the area, and he would stop in for coffee in the morning occasionally. His name was Rod Murchison, and his wife's name was Lucy. They became very good friends. One day, while chatting with Claire, he asked if she would come out to his house and help his wife with some decorating. Claire went and that is how she and Lucy became friends.

After Claire and Al got a buyer for their place, they talked to the owners of the half-acre lot. The owners made them an offer they couldn't refuse. If Claire and Al let them build the house, they would carry the paper on the mortgage with just the down payment Claire and Al had from the sale of their old place. So it was that they got a new house in the country.

While it was being built, Claire and Al rented a place above Claire and Barbara's store until school started; then, they rented a place in a little town called Baldwin Park, which was close to where they would build. They wanted to be nearby during the building. The boys enjoyed that. Jerry was just starting school; Alan was about ten years old.

Every night after work, Claire would go by to check the construction; often she would find things not as they wanted. One night when she went to check, she didn't like the quality of the baseboard wood, so she pulled it all out and left a note for them to replace it with the quality she wanted. Van Horn's son-in-law built a beautiful fireplace for them in the living room. When the house was completed, Claire furnished it beautifully, getting discounts through her associates in the furniture business.

One day Claire decided she wanted a wedding ring—which she had never gotten when they married—so she went to the Jewelry Mart to see a diamond setter who she met through Barbara Marshall. He was a sweet, little man by the name of Bert Sarna. While she was looking around, he showed her a ring he had just gotten in from an estate sale. He said, "The diamond in this ring is a European cut and very rare now." It was set in fourteen carat gold. Claire liked it, as the diamond was almost one carat in size. He gave her an affordable price, so Claire bought it. It was the first really nice piece of jewelry she ever had.

Claire was still working as an interior designer and attending a technical school to learn drafting. She was becoming more experienced and was doing well. She decided to get as much knowledge as she could since she knew she would always be working. Al worked at several jobs and was not happy with any of them, and none of them paid very well.

Her boys both played Little League baseball and loved it. The atmosphere on the home front was still not good. Al haggled about everything Claire did. It didn't just upset Claire, but other people too. Della, Al's sister, and her husband had curbed their visits because it embarrassed them to see how Al would talk and treat his wife. They always said it was uncalled for and they didn't like it, so they would not come unless it was a special occasion. Despite being Al's sister, Della always remained friends with Claire, even in later years.

In the meantime, Barbara became ill and couldn't work at the store. She discovered she had cancer, so they decided to close the store. One day while visiting the furniture mart, shopping for items for her clients, Claire met a woman who owned a furniture store with her husband in Pico Rivera, which was in East Los Angeles. She talked to Claire about coming to work for her as an interior designer. Claire thought about it and decided it was better pay, so she accepted the offer. The name of the store was "Abar's Furniture," Claire worked there for a couple of years. She became good friends with a lady who also came to work there whose name was Millie.

After working all day in the store, Claire would rush home to see the boys play ball. The mothers of the players were called the Women's Auxiliary, and they decided to form a little snack stand. They would call it the "Gee Dunk Stand," and they asked Claire to organize it since she was good at shopping. So she did. The first year, they made enough money to buy all the teams uniforms and replace some of the old equipment.

Eventually, Alan moved up into the Pony League, and Claire did the same for them. They finally made her president of the Women's Auxiliary for both Little League and Pony League and presented her with a pretty gavel to use when conducting the meetings. She still has that gavel.

Because Alan was so good at baseball, he received a scholarship to college. He decided to go to UCLA. The scouts were constantly after him to sign up for the major leagues. Finally, he told Claire he was going to drop out of college to do that. Claire was very disappointed and asked him not to. She said, "If they want you, they will wait until you are out of school." But, he quit anyway, and signed for the Angels club. Claire and Al would follow him to some of the places where he played at summer camp. She remembers they went to Pocatello once and saw him play.

He was a good center fielder. After traveling around with the farm team in summer camp for a couple of months, the Angels scheduled him to pitch for the team. Then he threw his arm out and had to sit on the bench. This he didn't like.

One night he called Claire and said he was coming home. He said he hadn't intended to join the team to just sit on the bench. He wanted to play ball, and he decided to quit. So he came home. After awhile he decided he didn't want to live at home anymore; he wanted to get his own place at the beach. By then he was old enough to work and be on his own. So he did. By then, Jerry was ready for junior college.

After working at Abar's for two years, Claire was referred to a man, Ed Ross, who wanted someone to manage his new store. Again, it would mean more money for Claire. It was a nice, modern furniture store. Claire went for the interview and accepted the job. This was in a little town called Bell.

Taking the job meant it was a long drive to work, and sometimes she was late getting home, so this would start another argument. She would still hurry home to see her boys play ball, and she worked the Gee Dunk stand, selling goodies to the players and fans.

It was about that time when Claire received a call from Rod and Lucy Murchison—the policeman and his wife who worked with Claire when she and Barbara had their store. They needed a decorator to do their new home on Linda Isle in Newport Beach. It was a very exclusive area on a private island. Claire contacted them and made an appointment to meet with them. They signed a contract with her to do the job, which took almost a year.

In the meantime, Rod Murchison had invested in some condos in Dana Point, south of Newport Beach, and he commissioned Claire to decorate the models. While he was involved in that venture, he met another woman, and that association brought trouble to his home life. Claire finished both the Linda Isle and the Dana Point job in spite of all the trouble.

Claire became so busy at the store with sales and decorating that she had to hire someone to assist her with the office work. She had a lot of responsibilities—arranging furniture, accepting shipments, making payroll for the workers, decorating for the clients. Claire liked one young woman who came in for an interview and hired her. Her name was Violet, but she said everyone called her "Vi." She was originally from Australia but had gone to Canada and married a man there and had a little girl. She had a difficult time because her husband did not want her to bring the little girl with her. But somehow she made it. The story of their escape, from Canada was related to Claire at a later date, by her daughter, Barbara, and it went like this:

When I was twelve years old, we boarded a Greyhound bus with seventeen pieces of luggage, each tied with a pink ribbon. I was responsible for the little green turtles in my purse, which I was allowed to bring because I had to leave the dog. Not understanding what it was like to ride in a bus, Mother dressed us both as if we were going to a play.

She cried when she described the things Father had said about her in his own defense. Her bruised eye had almost healed by the time we got to court, but the little dent cheekbone would be there for the rest of her life.

Mother had been working at the post office sorting letters and had been taking a course in book-keeping at night, so that when she left Father she would be able to make a good living. I think he figured this out. Mother and I moved to a rooming house after he hit her. That's when I had to leave the dog behind. We both lay in our beds at night and cry, she for her future and I for my dog.

Mother wanted to go to America because she had this idea, as all immigrants do, that she could make something of herself and maybe live the good life. The bus was to take us from Toronto, Canada, through the border at Detroit, and on across the country to Los Angeles, California. She heard that was where the flowers bloomed all year and we heard people were happy.

Since we were immigrating, the bus pulled over at the border crossing and Mother and I had to get out for customs inspection. We walked down the aisle, me clutching my turtles, Mother clutching her hat and tottering on high heels that she was not used to. The other people began asking, "What's going on? Why are we stopping?"

The bus driver, an impatient man with tinted glasses, yelled, "Shut up and sit down," and escorted us out of the bus and into the night. A hundred eyes peered out at us.

Mother was terrified. Her face was very white and the cheekbone with the little chip in it stood out. The bus driver motioned her to him and said in a low voice, "Look lady, I'm not pulling out seventeen pieces of luggage for them to inspect. When you go in there, you tell them you have two suitcases, no more." Her cheekbone began to twitch. "Do you understand what I'm saying , lady?" Mother nodded. She steered me to the door of the building.

Looking down she hissed, "You should have left those turtles on the bus."

We went into a big, bright room. We were the only ones there besides three cheerful men in uniforms who stood around talking. They were so different from the bus driver. I immediately felt encouraged and knew we had done the right thing coming to this country.

After a few minutes of checking and stamping papers, one of the uniformed men asked, "Where is your luggage?" Mother looked hunted. She didn't know what to say, but then the bus driver hurried in carrying two suitcases, pink ribbons dancing on the handles. He threw them up on the table, gave my mother a threatening look and, with hands on his hips he stayed to watch. The men grabbed the suitcases. In one was a giant, portable organ and the other, nothing but underwear. They considered the contents for a moment, then one asked, "Is this all you have?"

At that moment, Mother's cheekbone had a life of its own.

The bus driver interceded, "I'm on a schedule, Sir."

The man deliberated a moment, looked at the papers again, then at the organ and the underwear. Finally his eyes rested on Mother. Suddenly he beamed, "Well then, welcome to the United States!"

Claire liked Vi and hired her. Vi turned out to be a really good worker. She and her daughter were living in a one-room apartment at the time, and looking for a larger place. She finally found a little house that she could afford and liked, but she didn't have any furniture for it.

Claire decided to help her; she would have a house-warming party for Vi—everyone brought a piece of furniture. With this and with what Claire and Vi could dig up, the place was furnished enough to accommodate Vi and her daughter.

Alan was living at the beach with a couple of other boys, and Jerry was busy at junior college. For several years, Claire had been friends with a neighbor, Izzie, and on weekends and days off, they would go shopping or have lunch or do other things together. This didn't sit right with Al, and it started arguments. Whenever Claire did something Al didn't like or approve of, like going out with Izzie or coming home late from work, he would start an argument. He would keep haggling and stay on the subject until Claire would be completely stressed out, almost to tears. Clair and Al went out together occasionally, they would go to dinner at a restaurant close by, but when they did, it didn't end pleasantly.

One night, Claire's friend Millie suggested she, Al, and Claire go to the Elks Club nearby for dinner and cocktails. After the dinner, most of the crowd she knew gathered around the piano bar for singing, and soon they were requesting Claire to sing. All the while, Al kept nagging at Claire to go, but the crowd said, "No! Don't leave."

Soon the situation turned into an argument between Al and Claire and embarrassment for Claire, as the others looked at Claire with pity. Finally, Claire felt it was all she could take and said, "Alright we'll go, but this is it. There will be no more of this for me." She beckoned Millie to follow as they were leaving.

On the way home, Claire didn't say anything; she just thought to herself, why was she putting up with this? She had worked all these years to have a home and all the things they and the children wanted and needed. But they were grown now, and she didn't have to put up with this any longer.

She pulled into the driveway and waited for him to get out of the car, then drove off. She knew she didn't ever want to go back there. She didn't care if she ever saw that house again. She had put so much into it, but with so much unhappiness, to her it was not worth staying.

As she was taking Millie to her home, she said, "Millie, I don't want to go back there, but I don't know what to do. I'll need a place to live, and I will need to talk to my boys and see what they want to do. I know Alan is on his own now, but I need to get a place for me and Jerry."

Millie offered, "Claire you can move in with me until you find a place for you and Jerry."

A few days later, Claire talked to the boys and told them she just couldn't stay with their dad any longer and was moving out. They could decide if they wanted to stay there or go with her. She said, "I love you and no matter what you decide, I will still love you. No matter where I am, you can always come to me if you have a mind to do so. My home will always be open to you."

Alan planned to stay in the house at the beach. Jerry said, "Mom maybe I'll stay with Dad awhile, and maybe I can help him. I'm taking a psychology class in school, and maybe I can bring him some books from school." So Jerry stayed awhile.

Claire took all her clothing and some personal things when Al wasn't there. She knew Al would tear her up with his pleadings and accusations. She left the house and all its beautiful furnishings. Al could do whatever he wanted with it. She really didn't know how he could handle it all financially, but he didn't seem to appreciate all the effort she put into the house, pool and all. To her it was a price she had to pay for her happiness. She knew the boys were old enough now to be on their own. That is really what she waited so long for.

Claire stayed with Millie until she found a place she thought was suitable. She was still working at the furniture store in Bell and expected to see Al come around and cause trouble, but he didn't. Claire was thankful for that.

# Part Three

## AFTER THE DIVORCE

Vi was still working for Claire and things were very pleasant. Claire went out with Vi and her friends occasionally and enjoyed it. One day, a customer came into the store and Vi helped her—Claire was out with a client. The lady had a slight accent when she spoke, and it seemed she was from another country. The lady told Vi that she was looking for some furnishings for a friend of hers who was furnishing an office. She wanted to pick out some things she thought he might like. Just then, Claire returned, and Vi immediately turned her over to Claire. Claire showed the lady a few items that she thought would be good for an office. The lady liked them and made notes. She said she would tell her friend.

A few days later, Claire and Vi were busy arranging all the displays in the store. Claire sat down for a few minutes for a breather at her desk, which faced the front entrance. She located it there so she could greet the people as they entered. As she sat there, she noticed a large, black, shiny car pull up in front of the store. A man got out and came around the car to the store entrance and came in. He looked like someone very important, dressed like he stepped out of *Esquire Magazine*. He wore a sharp, black suit with a red vest and tie. He was a very handsome man.

He explained that his friend, Poppy, had been in earlier and found some things that he might like for his office. Claire proceeded to show him around and pointed out the items that his friend had picked out. He chose some things, but he wasn't sure. He asked if Claire would come to his office and help decorate it. Claire said yes. Of course, there would be a fee for her time, but he readily agreed to the charges. So she jotted down the appointment date and time, as well as his name and address. He had a very unusual name—Sigmund. It sounded like an important name to Claire.

His place was west of the store, about twenty miles north of Hollywood. It was a cute, little house. He had made an office out of the front bedroom. There were many bookcases containing lots of law books. Before he told her, Claire surmised he was an attorney. He was very mannerly and courteous. Claire liked the way he talked to her. She gave him a lot of ideas for his office, and he seemed quite receptive.

She helped him for couple of hours. When she began to leave, he asked her if he could visit her at the store again and take her to lunch. She replied, "Yes, if it can be someplace close to the store, because I can't be gone too long." He agreed, and they set a date.

After that, he came to the store frequently. Finally he asked her out for a dinner. He said he wanted to take her someplace really nice to show his gratitude. Claire had been replenishing her wardrobe with beautiful, up-to-date clothes, so she knew she would have just the right outfit for the occasion.

Claire was still living with Millie then, so she asked him to pick her up at the store. He took her to a very well-known, high-class Italian restaurant for dinner. She doesn't remember the entree, but she remembers they had demitasse in cute, little cups. Sig asked her if she liked them, and she said, yes, so when the waiter came back to the table, he bought the demitasse cups and gave them to Claire. That was the beginning of a beautiful love story.

The next time he asked to take her out, he took her to the Beverly Hills Hotel for lunch. Afterwards, they strolled around the lobby, window shopping in the exclusive shops. In one window a mannequin was holding a beautiful fan. Sig asked her if she would like the fan. She thought he was kidding. They agreed that it was very beautiful, so he walked into the shop and bought it for Claire. There were many more lunches and dinners with Sig. He always took her to elite places and pampered her.

She was beginning to fall for this man. He was a prince to her. He caressed her like she had always wanted to be caressed, so gentle and sweet. He invited her to his place often and insisted she sit and allow him to wait on her. He would serve her wine in beautiful crystal stemware, and Claire noticed that everything he had was the best. He seemed to enjoy pampering her and liked to take her shoes off and rub and kiss her feet. He treated her with such endearment that they often retreated to the bedroom. It seemed that his concern was always Claire. This was the kind of caring that Claire hungered for.

Sig had a friend who was in the diamond business. He would often bring Claire a beautiful, expensive piece of diamond jewelry. One time it was a fourteen carat gold pin with diamonds and rubies made in the shape of a roadrunner. Once, it was a ring with a beautiful, pale yellow stone called a citrine. Claire had never seen one like it. Then he began to give her diamond rings set in platinum. One ring was set with many baguette diamonds, and it was gorgeous. Each gift overshadowed the last. Finally he gave her a diamond ring with Marquise cuts and baguettes in it. Some of them were set in the shape of a "C." It was also set in platinum. Claire treasured it.

This went on and on for months, and Claire was falling more and more in love with Sig. But was it love or appreciation for all the affection and gifts he was showering on her?

One day, as Claire was coming back to the store from Sig's office, she was driving on the freeway and in the traffic ahead, two lanes to the right, she could see a tow truck pulling another truck backwards. Suddenly, one of the wheels came off the disabled truck and headed straight for Claire's car. Claire tried to turn away, towards the center divider, but the wheel kept coming at her. Finally, it hit the front of her car, causing the car to go up in the air and simply ride the wheel. Then her car came down with a terrific crash. It just jarred her something awful. After the police arrived, she immediately called Sig, the only person who was on her mind. She didn't feel hurt at the time.

But afterwards, Claire went through months of agony with terrible head pains. At first she thought it was just regular headaches, until the pains became much worse. All the while, Sig insisted she go to a chiropractor, but Claire never had much faith in that kind of a doctor. Finally, after taking all kinds of pain pills, and even alcohol, she took Sig's suggestion. As the chiropractor worked on her, she thought she was going to die of the pain. But, after three or four visits, he corrected the problem. She will never forget his name—Dr. Elmer Bones.

When Claire found out her car was totaled, Sig suggested she lease a Cadillac, which he said might be better for her new job, and she decided to do that. She was still working at the store in Bell, but her boss was thinking of selling it. He had another store just down the street where he sold only Colonial maple furniture. He didn't need both.

Vi left the store to take a better job at Gaffers & Sattler, a company that made kitchen ranges. She had become pretty good at book work, and Claire gave her a good reference.

In the meantime, Ted Richards, the owner of another store where Claire shopped for appliances and brands of furniture she couldn't get at her store, offered her a job as a decorator. Since Ed Ross was thinking of closing up his store, she accepted the offer.

She knew she would need an apartment or something on that side of town. Sig suggested she move in with him, but she declined that offer. After searching, she found an apartment not too far from him. It was very nice, close to her job, and Claire furnished it beautifully.

Her sons would call her from time to time and tell her what was going on with their dad. He was not doing very well financially. One day, Jerry called her and said he couldn't live with him any longer because he couldn't put up with his actions. He said Al was drinking a lot and giving away or selling all the beautiful things in the house in order to buy beer. There were a few things that Jerry liked, and he hated to see his dad give them away. He said he was going to quit school and get a job.

Claire was not happy about him leaving school, but decided she really couldn't do much about it. Claire told Jerry he could come and stay with her if he wanted to. She introduced him to Sig, and they seemed to get along well. Sig told Jerry that if he really wanted to go to work, he would ask his friend Poppy to get Jerry a job with her in a metallurgist lab. Poppy was a chemist. She did get him a job there.

While Jerry was still living with his dad, his car broke down, and he was without wheels. He needed a car for transportation. He tried to buy one on his own, but couldn't. Sig came to his rescue and offered to co-sign for Jerry. After that, they became friends. Jerry always said he liked Sig.

Finally, Jerry came to stay with Claire for a little while, but then he decided to go and live with Alan at the beach. He quit his job at the lab and got a job with the phone company. Then, he went into computers and worked in that field for a long time.

One day, Al called Claire and told her he was getting a divorce. That was a relief to Claire. He also said he was getting remarried—to his attorney's secretary—and asked if she would sign the divorce papers. Needless to say, Claire was happy for him and happy for herself.

Things were still very thick between Claire and Sig. He was at her place most of the time. She would regularly prepare evening meals for them. She also had a key made for him. Things went on like that for almost a year.

Claire was happy with Sig. She knew she had fallen in love with him, and she believed he was in love with her. He was always there when she came home from work. He continued to shower her with beautiful things, such as diamond rings and broaches, and took her to elegant places. Claire was always dressed to the "nth," as he was. She was making good money now, and she could afford beautiful clothing and accessories.

Claire met a girl named Carol who lived downstairs, and they often spent time together, swimming or talking. She was from England and was on her own too. She was very nice. They became good friends and remained friends for years. Sometimes Sig would come to Claire's place and swim with them.

Then Sig began to stay away for several days at a time. Claire would come home from work and expect him to be there, but he wasn't. She realized she had really fallen in love with Sig, and this troubled her.

Distracted, Claire suddenly discovered her monthly period had not stopped. After a month, she told Millie who immediately took Claire to a gynecologist. The doctor put her into the hospital for a D&C (a cleansing procedure). He thought she may have been pregnant and lost it, but not completely. He said the D&C should clear it up.

While she was in the hospital, her doctor discovered a small lump in her breast. After examining it further, he said they would need to operate. Claire asked, "Do you think you will need to remove the breast?"

He said, "If it need be." Claire went into shock.

That afternoon, the doctor came in to her again and explained that there was a German specialist visiting the hospital, and he wanted him to examine Claire. After the examination, the specialist suggested that a simple aspiration might resolve the situation. If the lump went away, she would not require surgery, which is what happened. Claire was so relieved. She was told that her doctor had put her on estrogen too early and at too strong a dose, a practice that causes nodules to form. Sig came to visit at the hospital several times, always late at night.

Claire was becoming depressed about Sig staying away so much, for so long. She was beginning to think perhaps he was involved in something illegal, and she tried to figure out what it could be.

After this ordeal was over, Sig took Claire to Palm Springs for a weekend holiday. He made reservations at the finest hotel and appointments for Claire at a spa so she could have massages and facials and all the beauty procedures that were available. They had a wonderful time. One night, at dinner, an artist was approaching people asking to draw and paint their portraits. Sig insisted he draw Claire, but Claire was not very happy about having a picture painted. She was feeling depressed about Sig's continued absences. He said he wanted to hang it in his house, so she agreed. He would always do things like that, and it impressed Claire

Claire became increasingly nervous about their relationship. Night after night, she would not see him. She would be upset, and her heart would pound. Where can he be? Is he out with someone else? Is he taking someone to his place? So Claire would get in her car and go check it out.

One time he disappeared for five or six days. He wasn't at her place or his place. Claire was really upset. She thought all kinds of things. He must have someone else. When he finally returned, she confronted him. But he just said he was away and couldn't tell her where or anything about it. He said if she knew what he was doing, and someone questioned her, she would have to tell them, and he didn't want that to happen.

The next time he left for several days Claire decided she would change the locks on her door so his key wouldn't fit. She decided if he was going to play around with other women, she didn't want to be available to him. So she changed the locks on the doors of her apartment. Claire had told the landlady about the situation and she understood. She also asked her not to let Sig in, if he came there. The landlady told Claire later that she saw Sig try to get into the apartment one afternoon and couldn't. She wouldn't give him a key, per Claire's instructions, and he was furious.

One night, when he didn't answer the telephone, Claire drove to his house. She saw his car there, as well as another car she didn't recognize. She went to the door and rang the bell. She could hear the music inside, but no one came to the door. As she stood there, she became more and more nervous and suspicious. She called out to him, but he didn't answer. Finally, she yelled, "Sig, if you have someone else, just give me that painting of me and I will leave." She didn't want him flaunting her picture to other women. This went on for hours, but Claire wouldn't leave.

Finally he called out to her and told her to go home—he was not giving her the painting. This made her furious and she began to cry. She knew he had someone else in there, and it broke her heart more than she could bear. If he was tired of her, why didn't he tell her he wanted to break it off instead of doing things to make her love him more as time went on? She decided she would stay there, on that step, until he gave her the painting.

It was getting late and dark and cold. She was glad she had brought her mink coat. She wrapped it around her and prepared to stay all night. She didn't know how long it was before she saw a police car pull up in front of the house. A policeman came up to her and asked her what she was doing. She said through her tears, "I just came to get my painting from this man, and he won't give it to me"

"Is the painting yours?" he asked

Claire said, "Yes!"

So the policeman knocked on the door and Sig came out. Then the policeman said to Sig, "Why don't you just give her the painting and she will go away?"

Sig walked back into the room and took the painting off the wall where it hung over the stereo. He came back out and handed it to Claire.

Claire could see the other woman in the living room, so she just turned around and put the painting in her car and left. Her heart was broken. She lay awake all night crying. The next day when she got to work, she didn't know how she would get through the day. As she was standing behind the counter she began to feel weak and dizzy. One of the other salespersons grabbed her. Then her boss came out and told her to take the rest of the day off. She called Alan at the beach. He was at work, but his girlfriend came and picked Claire up and took her to Alan's place.

The next day her boss said to her, "You better go and see your friend, the travel agent, and make arrangements to go on a trip, anywhere, to get this off your mind. You can't work until your mind is clear of this." He thought a trip would be good for her.

The next day, Claire went to her travel agent friend. After talking and planning with him awhile he said, "You know, Claire, I have something you might like. A golfing group has chartered a flight to Portugal, and there are a couple of empty seats available on the plane. I think I could get a very good price for you on that trip. How would you like that?"

It sounded good to Claire, and as it turned out, he was able to get a very good price. She began to plan her trip abroad. Each day she would become more excited. She had never gone on a long trip like this before. She thought some fun and good times would help her forget everything she had just gone through.

She called her sons to tell them, and Alan informed her he was taking off for Hawaii at the same time.

Finally the day of departure came. They flew north, and she saw the Aurora Borealis over the North Pole, which was magic to her. Their first stop was Paris. It was a long flight, but she became acquainted with the entire group, and they had a ball. Claire became buddy-buddies with one of the girls, Dolly. In Paris, Claire and Dolly went to see the Eiffel Tower and went to the top. That was strange since the elevator went up at an angle. They also went to the Moulin Rouge and did lots of sightseeing. The hotel was right across from the Moulin Rouge. It was a very old hotel. The bathrooms were so old that the bathtubs were perched on legs in the middle of the room, and the toilets were flushed by chains. And there was an old-fashioned bidet.

One night Dolly and Claire and a couple other girls decided they wanted to go out, but they didn't know where to go. Dolly and Claire thought they would just walk around and check it all out. They left the hotel and started down a narrow street (all the streets were narrow). The name of this street was Rue Lafontaine. They didn't know if these buildings were residences or businesses. There were no porches or lobbies or any other entryways into the buildings. There were just doors on the brick walls with a single light on one side. There were many like that. One of the doors had a little sign on the side that read, "Charleston Club Discotheque," so the girls all decided it must have something to do with music or entertainment. There was a door bell, but the other girls were afraid to ring the bell.

Claire said, "I'll do it; let's go see what they have."

She rang the bell, and in a few seconds, the little peep-hole opened and a face said, "May I help you?"

Claire said, "We thought this was a bar or something"

He responded, "Yes, it's a bar and a discotheque. Would you like to come in?" He opened the door and let them in, and as they stood inside, he asked them to wait—he would be right back. When he returned, he explained that this was a club, and the owner was "Les" something or other. As they looked around, they noticed that some of the women looked a little bit like men, and they came to the conclusion it was a drag club. He escorted them to a table on the small balcony. He told them that the owner said they would like that table because they could see better from there. When he took their order for drinks, he told them that the owner would join them shortly.

As the girls were taking in the sights, a very handsome man came over to their table and introduced himself as Les. He asked where they were from and they said, California. He said he owned the place and was an impersonator. He said he was from California too and had been an impersonator in San Francisco for several years.

He heard that the "drag" business was very good in Paris, so he moved and opened this place. He showed them a picture of himself made up as a very beautiful woman. It turned out that his name and the name of the club was "Les-Lee's."

The owner and all of his staff were very courteous to the girls. And the girls were so interested in the place that they decided they would come back the next night. They enjoyed watching the crowd dancing and seeing how they were made up. Some of them were very beautiful.

The next night, Dolly and Claire went there without the other girls. They were ushered to the same table and told that the owner would join them again. They ordered their drinks, and Les soon joined them. He asked what they did in California. Dolly told him she was in real estate. Claire told him she was an interior decorator. He seemed to relate to that. He told them about his life in California. He said that he had married and had a daughter there. He decided to change his lifestyle, so he began to impersonate a woman, and got a job in a drag discotheque in San Francisco. That's when his marriage ended. He told them that he still liked women and that he had a girlfriend in Paris. His drag name was Les-Lee. For Claire and Dolly, the two evenings were very interesting.

The next day, the group moved on to another interesting place. They traveled on a bus to Evian, which was in the French Alps. It was a beautiful place in the mountains with a famous golf course (for the golfing group). They all stayed at a lovely chateau-style inn called the LaVerniaz. It was very European.

In the evenings, everyone gathered in the dining room for dinner. After dinner, they all filed into the bar where the music was playing. Claire was sitting at the bar when two very nice older men came up to her. One sat on her left, and the other sat on her right. They were both trying to win Claire over. One of them, "Bobbee," was from Brittany. He said he owned a golf course there and came to Evian for golf matches. He was a real sweet man. He joined her every night. He didn't seem to want to leave her alone. One day, he said he wanted to take her to meet his sister who lived in Geneva. Claire went with him and he drove her to Geneva, Switzerland, which was not very far away. His sister lived in a little flat which was styled in a very Swiss flavor.

Claire had a nice time meeting the sister and dining with them. Bobbee told his sister that he was going to go to America and marry Claire. His sister said it was fine with her. When Claire left Evian, he asked for her address and said he would be in touch with her. Claire didn't think she would ever hear from him again, but she gave him her address anyway.

Then they went on to Nice. On the way there, Dolly was telling Claire about a little village she had read about. It sounded very interesting to them. The following morning, they invited a local girl, who seemed to know where this little village was located, to guide them. She said to them, "There is no public transportation to that area, but it isn't too far; we could walk there."

The three of them started out walking. When they had walked a couple of miles, an elderly man in an old car stopped and offered them a ride. They told him that they were tourists and wanted to see the village, which they had read about.

He said, "It is a few miles further up the mountain and if you would like, I can take you back when you are ready. I will be going back to Nice later, also." They thanked him for the offer and entered the village.

When the girls entered the village, they couldn't believe their eyes. It was so beautiful. Everything was built with stone—the entry and the buildings, the stone steps and the walkways leading to the upper floors. There were small, quaint, shuttered windows in each of the living quarters, above. The bottom floors were all shops. At the gate of the entry was a large, beautiful fountain. This was so picturesque that they didn't know what to look at first. They went up a walkway to the second floor, looking into the small, vacant apartments. They came upon a very pretty woman, sitting at the entry to one of the living quarters. She didn't pay much attention to them. She just continued with her reading.

As they walked away, the local girls asked, "Do you know who that was?"

Claire responded, "She did look familiar."

The girl said, "That was Simone Simon. Do you remember her?" Claire and Dolly did. The girl explained to them, "This is a village hide-a-way, where many of the well-known actors and actresses come to get away from the public and live in seclusion."

Soon they went down to the entry and waited for the motorist, to see if he would really come back. He did, and he took them to Nice.

The next stop for the group was Monte Carlo, where they only stayed for the day. On the way there, they stopped in Cannes and visited a gambling casino. They also visited a couple of casinos near the city of Monte Carlo, which was up on a very high mountain.

They all got quite a kick out of the casinos because it was very different than the casinos in California and Las Vegas. When they walked in, you could hear a pin drop. There was no noise allowed and no talking. It was quieter than a library. At the least little noise someone would go, "Shhhshish."

The next day, the group leader chartered a bus to Lisbon. That was where they wanted to go next. That was a very interesting trip. They had the bar set up in the bus, and all the way down, they had a party. There were all kinds of refreshments.

They got to see lots of the country. There were "cork trees," which Claire had never seen before. They stopped at a little, old residential home where they were served a luncheon outside in a dirt yard under the trees with the peacocks running around like chickens. The people were very gracious and humble. It didn't seem as though they had much, but they wanted to show their hospitality. It was very interesting for Claire to see some of the furniture designs in the homes and how they were being used.

Portugal was a very clean country; all of the walkways and curbs were painted white. They were told that the government made them keep it that way.

They finally arrived at a place on the ocean, the Hotel Praia Da Roche. It was a lovely, modern hotel. They were all assigned to their rooms in pairs, but because Claire had made her reservations on her own, she was assigned a private room. They all planned to meet down in the lounge after they showered and dressed.

When Claire walked in, the men in her group all whistled. That embarrassed Claire a little. She was wearing her beautiful silver lame trench coat covering a luscious, turquoise sheer, palazzo suit. The waiter took their order, but the bartender delivered the drinks. Wow! Claire thought, he is really cute.

Claire asked, "What happened to our waiter?"

"Well," he said in a definite Portuguese or Spanish accent, smiling directly at Claire, "You see, here in Portugal, the owner may deliver the order if he feels the customers are special, and I think you are special."

As he walked away, the group all heckled Claire and told her she had better watch out or she was going to have an admirer. Every time he came over to the group he seemed to give Claire special attention. Soon, Claire was getting a thrill out of his attentions.

The following night was the same, except when he came over to them, he sat next to her and put his arm on her shoulder. He became friendly with the entire group, and they all enjoyed talking to him about the area, including the golfing. When the group decided to retire, Claire asked the waiter if she could order a nightcap to take to her room. He returned to the bar, and soon the owner/bartender, Arturo, came to her and said, "We will bring the drink to your room."

Claire thanked him and departed with the rest of the group. When she got in her room and was removing her coat, there came a tap on the door. When she opened the door, there was Arturo with the drink on a tray.

"I thought the waiter was going to bring it up," she said.

"Well, I wanted to see you again," he said. "You are very lovely."

As they stood there with the door open, Claire offered him a gratuity, which he refused.

He asked, "May I come in? You see, I am not supposed to patronize with the customers, and I'd rather they didn't see me."

Claire couldn't allow him to come in as she didn't know him well, but she said, "I'm sorry, I do appreciate your delivering the drink," and she bid him good-night. As Claire closed the door, she was bewildered. She didn't know what to think. He was so charming and handsome. He seemed to be very attracted to Claire and of course, after the disappointment she had just experienced, she was ready for any compliments.

Claire talked to Dolly about him, and Dolly thought it was great if it gave her good feelings. The next night was a repeat of the night before. She didn't order a drink delivered this time, but he brought it to her anyway. Again, she didn't invite him in. In the few nights that followed, when they would meet in the lounge, he was increasingly amorous and embraced Claire often. He didn't seem to be aware of the rest of the group, and they seemed to expect him to be there now.

Finally, when he delivered her drink one night and asked if he could come in, just for a minute, Claire agreed. He seemed very happy and excited. When he entered the room, he grabbed her and kissed her passionately, and Claire responded. Then they came back to reality and sat and talked. Claire said she wanted to know more about him. He told her how the hotel leased the bar to him and that he was married and had two children, but his wife and children lived somewhere other than Portugal.

He asked Claire if she had ever been to Spain. Claire replied, "No."

Then he said, "I have a couple of vacation days coming, and I would like to take you to "Seviya" (Sevilla) and show you the beauty of Spain. It would be a very nice trip; we would go on a barge, and we could spend the day there. You will not need to worry; I will be a gentleman and treat you like a lady."

The next day when Claire saw him, he said he could get away for a few hours, and since the rest of the group were out playing golf, he asked if she would like to see the Lagos. Of course, Claire didn't know what the Lagos was. He explained that it was a lot of caves and rock arch formations offshore. People go by boat and row in and out of them. So she accepted the invitation, and they went out on the boat and had a wonderful time. He could not have been nicer to her.

He still continued to talk about taking her to Seville, Spain. She had become so flattered by his attentions that she began to think seriously about going with him. He was such a doll; she was sure she wouldn't need to worry. So, she decided that if he asked her again, she would accept, and he did. She had no idea how far it was or how long it would take. Arturo turned out to be a true gentleman and mannerly.

They took a barge over the water to Spain. When they landed, he hired a car and he drove her all around to see the sights. They spent the rest of the day sight-seeing. When night came, he said, "We'd better get a room for the night. I'll get a room for you, and I'll stay someplace else." Claire asked where he would stay.

"I have friends here. I'll pick you up in the morning, and we'll do a little more sight-seeing." he replied. Claire thought that perhaps his wife and children were there, and he would stay with them.

Then he took Claire in his arms in a loving embrace and kissed her passionately as if he didn't want to let her go. After some very nice love-making (with precautions taken), he left.

The next morning, he was there to pick her up, and they had breakfast at a sidewalk café. Then they boarded a tier bus, and they rode around to see more sights, taking snapshots of interesting places. Finally, they boarded the barge and took more photos and headed back. When they arrived at the hotel, they split up before entering, as Claire knew her new friends would be wondering where she had been. Dolly knew, but she didn't tell anyone.

As it came time for Claire to leave, Arturo became very sad. He told Claire he would write to her and maybe try to come to California. Claire knew that would not happen, so she was very sad too, but glad that she had such a wonderful time with him.

The next morning everyone said good-bye, and Arturo embraced Claire and gave her a very warm kiss before they all piled in the bus, headed for Lisbon. From there they were taking a plane back to Paris for the trip home.

On the plane to Paris, Claire began to forget about Arturo. The steward on the plane was very European and talked to Claire all the way to Paris. He asked for her address and said he would write to her. He gave her a post card with a picture of the plane, with him on it. Claire didn't think she would ever hear from him, but three weeks later she received a letter from him. Claire decided not to answer it.

After they left Paris, they made a stop in Shannon, Ireland. She didn't know why, perhaps for some kind of repairs or fuel.

They spent a couple of hours there, and it was all spent in an Irish pub. They all had fun with a group of Irish drinkers. They wanted to keep Claire there. She had so much fun with them.

Finally, she was back home and back to work. That was the end of a wonderful vacation, which she would never forget. She did receive a telegram from Bobbee of Brittany, France, saying he was going to make plans to come to her, but she never heard anymore She also received several loving letters from Arturo, and after a time they too dwindled down. It was a geographically undesirable relationship.

Her attention turned to her work, and she became very busy with clients. In addition, she and Dolly began a hobby of making handbags out of men's metal lunch pails. They would paint designs on the outside of the pails and line the inside with fabric, then sell them. That was fun for Claire.

In the meantime, Claire was looking for a new place to move from her apartment—she thought it was too close to Sig. She became friends with one of her clients, Rosemary. They would lunch together and go to dinner together. She was a widow and had a grown son and daughter. She was a member of the Levi jeans family. She lived in Beverly Hills and knew of a small apartment where one of her male friends was living. It was just a studio, but Claire didn't think she needed more than that. So she rented it.

That was where she lived when the big earthquake in Simi Valley occurred. The refrigerator, on one side of the room slid over to the other side of the room and all of her food came out, pouring ketchup and mayonnaise all over the room. Dishes broke and pictures fell off the walls. She was scared.

About that time, Claire decided to take a trip to Hawaii. She had been corresponding with her Alan, who had moved there. He was always encouraging her to come over there for a visit. So one day she made plans to do just that. She went to her travel agent and he made all the arrangements for her trip. It was to be a ten-day trip on three islands: two days in Kona; three days in Oahu at the Kahala-Hilton Hotel; and five days with Alan on Kauai.

When she was in Kona, she stayed at the Kona Inn where all the fishermen stayed, and she had a lot of fun with them when they came in from a fishing trip. She would meet them in the bar and have a ball. They were lots of fun.

When she arrived on Oahu, the hotel was beautiful, but she had nothing to do as this was a brand new hotel with nothing close by. So she called Alan, and he asked how she was enjoying things. Claire said, "Everything is beautiful, but I'm bored, so why don't you come over here, and we can do something together?"

Alan said, "That sounds good, but can I bring Leland with me?" Leland was his friend.

"Of course. I have a large suite here with extra sleeping facilities in the living room," Claire responded.

So they came over, and Claire and the two boys had a ball. They went out to all the discos they could find and danced up a storm. They stayed a couple of days.

When she got to Kauai, Alan took her to his place, a little teahouse among a jungle of trees and plants. He was working for the man who owned the property. Claire couldn't believe how well Alan had decorated this little place. No one would believe it unless they saw it. It was so cute.

On the way to his place from the airport, Alan said, "Mom I've met a very nice girl. Her name is Terry, and I'm sure you'll like her. She's very sweet and mellow. She'll be staying with us. I'll pick her up from the airport tomorrow."

His girl did come and as Alan promised, she was very sweet. It rained the entire time Claire was there, but Alan and Terry tried their best to show Claire a good time. They took her to a resort to acquaint her with the local music and hula dances. In spite of all the rain, Claire did enjoy the visit very much.

Then it was back to California and work.

It was several weeks later that Claire received a call again from Alan. He was in town with his girlfriend and wanted to show her around—the places where he grew up, went to school and lived. He called Claire to let her know.

Then he said, "Mom, are you singing anyplace now? We would like to come and hear you."

Claire said, "Well, I'll be at Murphy's Bar and Restaurant tonight if you would like to come." They came and had cocktails with Claire. When Claire was asked to sing, she went to the microphone on the dance floor and belted out a song for them. They couldn't believe their ears. Alan stood up, with watery eyes and grabbed Claire with a hug and said, "Mom, I can't believe what we just heard. I never knew you could sing like that. He had never heard her sing publicly. They both were surprised.

One night after they had dinner together, her friend Rosemary suggested they go to the West Lake Hotel, which featured a band and dancing, for an after-dinner drink. As she and Claire were enjoying the drink and the music, the waitress served them the second drink. They gave the waitress a surprised look, and the waitress said as she pointed, "That is from the gentleman over there." Claire saw the gentleman and gave him a nod to thank him. Rosemary and Claire returned to their conversation.

In a few minutes, the gentleman approached their table and introduced himself as James. Then he looked straight at Claire and said, "Would you have this dance with me?" Claire took another look at him. Although he was good-looking, he was also over six feet tall. She knew she would look like a midget dancing with him, but she didn't want to embarrass him.

Claire looked at Rosemary as if to say, I don't think it's nice to leave you alone at the table. Rosemary motioned to Claire to go and dance with him. He was very nice and mannerly. He said he was a minister of a church in Oklahoma.

After requesting a few more dances, he asked if he could see Claire again, and would she agree to give him her phone number? She agreed and jotted it down on a napkin. That was the beginning of another unusual friendship.

Her bosses decided to open an additional store in the city of Hawthorne and asked Claire to transfer to the new store. She agreed, but she'd need to find a new place to live in that area. She found a cute apartment, and she decorated it real cute with lots of yellows and whites, adding some pieces of chrome furniture.

Claire was still seeing Jim.

While working at the new store in Hawthorne, her bosses decided to hire an assistant. She was a pretty, little Eurasian girl, as cute as can be. She seemed to bring in the male customers, which was good for business. She tried hard to learn about decorating and before long, she did.

One day, a friend of hers came in and was introduced to Claire. She was more Claire's age, and Claire liked her. Her name was Geraldine, and they called her Geri. She was separated from her husband, but they both lived in separate parts of the same house. Claire thought this was funny. She would become a lifelong friend of Claire's.

After Claire went out with Jim two or three times, he became very amorous. Claire began to like him very much. He was so sweet to her. One night as they were in a very passionate embrace, he began to reveal a few of his personal problems to her. She believed him, as he seemed very sincere.

He said he was married and that his wife had alienated their marriage. He told her that one day, when he returned home unexpectedly, he found her in bed with another man. He then discovered through neighbors and friends that this had been going on for some time. Because of the embarrassment, he decided to leave town and think over what to do.

Claire decided there had to be two sides to the story, and this was only one side. That didn't change Claire's feelings for him. She still liked him and wanted to be with him. She needed all the love she could get and would accept all he was willing to give. She adored the attention and love he gave her, but sometimes Claire didn't see him for weeks. Then he would show up and call and ask to see her. This went on for months, and each time he was more amorous.

One time, he asked her to meet him at the airport and spend a night or two with him when he was scheduled to return from one of his trips. Claire made reservations at the Sheridan Hotel by the airport, and he gave her his return date. While she was at the hotel waiting for him, he called and said his return time was delayed, but he still intended to meet her there.

Claire didn't feel like she wanted to stay there and wait for him alone. Maybe he wouldn't show up at all, she thought, and she had the room reserved, so why not call her friend Geri and see if she would come and join her. They could enjoy the pool and have some fun at the hotel.

She called Geri, and Geri agreed to meet Claire at the hotel. That night before Claire heard from Jim again, she and Geri decided to go down to the pool and spa before they had dinner. They had just gotten in the spa when a couple of guys came along and joined them. After talking to one another and having a lot of laughs, the two guys started to make a play for both of them. They wanted them to come to their rooms. Of course Geri and Claire refused. They made remarks suggesting that Claire and Geri were lesbians. Claire and Geri just laughed. Finally, they asked if the girls had dinner yet. Geri and Claire explained that they were waiting for Claire's friend to meet them. Of course, the men didn't know whether that meant a male or female, and they didn't ask. So they invited Claire and Geri to join them for dinner. They took the girls to a very nice restaurant where they had a very pleasant dinner.

When they returned to the hotel, they were under the impression then that Claire and Geri would go to their room with them, but the girls refused. While they were in the lobby, Jim showed up, and they were introduced to him. That changed the whole scene. The men disappeared, Geri departed for home, and Claire and Jim went to their room.

Time went on, and Claire was busy in the decorating business. One day, as she returned from a client's project, her boss handed her a note for another job to handle. He said some guy called and requested that a decorator come out to his place to help him decorate his condo.

Her boss said, "This guy sounded foreign, sort of Italian, so be careful. He left his phone number for you." Claire said she would take care of it.

Claire called the number, and she could tell he was Italian. She made an appointment to go to his condo. When she met him and gave him some quotes, he hired her to do the job. He seemed like a nice fellow, short and very strong looking, and mannerly in his Italian way. His name was Salvatore (a nice Italian name).

After Claire had met with him several times, and they had gotten very friendly, he asked to take her out for dinner and dancing. She went with him, and they did this several times. She was really enjoying being with him. One night, after several drinks and much dancing, they returned to Sal's place. The drinks were beginning to hit Claire, and she became very sleepy and flopped on the sofa. In her stupor, she became aware that Sal was making love to her, and she was accepting him. She had not had that feeling since she had been with Sig. This made her feel alive again.

A holiday was drawing near, and he insisted that she and some of her friends, including her son Jerry, come over to his place for dinner. It was to be an Italian dinner. Claire was to help him prepare it. He was going to show her how to cook Italian food. Everyone enjoyed being there and had a good time and seemed to like him.

After that, it became a regular affair, and they became very close. The more Claire was with him, the more she liked him. He also seemed to be smitten with her. He never seemed to hold back his advances when anyone was present. When they were alone, he became more loving, and it would end up very passionate, in an Italian sort of way. Claire yearned for that.

Sal corresponded with his family in Philadelphia regularly, and his sister Christina decided to come to California and meet Claire. Sal and Christina decided it should be a permanent affair. Although it became more serious, Claire didn't feel that this should be a permanent affair.

She liked Sal, but she still wanted to go out with other male friends. Sal was jealous, just like a typical Italian lover.

While Claire was still seeing Sal, she occasionally saw Jim, as well. He would call and ask if he could take her out to dinner or dancing, and she would accept. Sal was more attentive, but it was not convenient for him to be with her as he worked as a hair stylist in Beverly Hills.

She was getting along fine in her new place of work, picking up new clients. It didn't dawn on her then, but as she looks back, it seems that she met a lot of people through this business; people who were to become more attached to her during an important episode in her life.

At that time, Gloria, the new decorator, was having problems with her spouse at home, so she wasn't very happy. She and her husband had two children. One boy was her husband's by a former marriage, and they had a girl together. She finally decided to leave him and move into the complex where Claire lived. It was close to work for both Claire and Gloria.

Gloria, Geri and Claire would go out on the town, and they had so much fun together. Whenever they did, it seemed that all the men headed for Gloria, as she was a pretty little thing with long, dark hair. Geri and Claire got a kick out of that because they knew she was a big flirt.

Sometimes Gloria and Geri would go out together without Claire and get into a little trouble. One time they met a couple of guys who were attorneys. As Claire understood it, one of them had an airplane and decided to take them for a flight. Neither Gloria nor Geri knew the men very well, but they both accepted. They flew to Riverside to a condo there where they stayed the night. The guys wanted them to go into the bedrooms with them. But Geri said, "I'm sorry, but I will sleep on the sofa." She was supposed to go to work the next morning and so was Gloria. Whether the guys got what they wanted, Claire never knew. They did get back in time for their work. When Claire saw Gloria, she looked like she had been drawn through a knot hole. Geri told Claire it was scary.

Claire knew of a little Italian restaurant in Beverly Hills with a piano bar. She had gone there several times earlier and sat at the bar and sang with the piano player. She loved to do that. When she was a little girl she always wanted to be a singer. This seemed to fill that void for her. Claire would take Geri there many times, and they always had an enjoyable evening.

One night Claire, Geri and Gloria decided to go there, and Gloria invited a friend to join them. On the way, they passed a private disco club and stopped to see if they could go in. Gloria got out of the car to inquire. At first the answer was no, but after a few minutes of talking, she went in. Well! The three of them sat and waited for her to return, and they waited and waited. Claire said, "I don't think it's nice of Gloria to desert her friends. If she wants to stay, let her, but we're going. She'll need to find her own way there."

So Claire drove off and left her. Gloria had one of the guys from the disco bring her to the restaurant. They were all sitting at the piano bar singing and in came Gloria with this guy. Claire and Geri laughed and laughed. Gloria never left the other girls again. They ended up that night having a good time.

Another night, when Geri and Claire went to the same restaurant to sit at the piano bar and sing, two guys came on strong. Claire was sitting on one side of the piano bar singing her heart out, and Geri was on the other side. Geri really seemed to go for the guy whose name was Forest. The other guy was George, who Geri met there at another time. When it was closing time, they asked if they could take Geri and Claire to breakfast (as it was now early in the morning). George liked Geri, but she wanted to be with Forest, so that was arranged. It didn't make any difference to Claire who she was with as she had a good time singing. George still hung on to Geri and finally made a date with her.

It was a nice breakfast, and they sat there a long time getting acquainted. Finally, Claire said they had better break it up as they needed to go to work the next morning. Geri's escort, Forest, asked if he could take her home. He didn't have any idea how far it was, but he insisted, and she agreed. Claire said goodnight to George and left. Geri was staying with Claire that night. She waited for her for hours. It was raining that night. Finally, Geri arrived. Apparently, Forest was a good lover, and they enjoyed sitting in the car kissing for hours while it poured rain. It appeared that he didn't want to leave her.

Geri finally separated from her husband and got her own apartment close to her job as a dental assistant.

One beautiful day, as Claire and Geri were sitting by the pool, they could see a gentleman holding a large bouquet of flowers in the entrance to the complex. Claire couldn't believe her eyes. There was her wonderful Sig. He was such a handsome man. As usual, he was sharply dressed, looking very much like George Hamilton. He handed her the flowers and said he wanted to talk to her. She accepted the bouquet and headed for her apartment to put them in water. When they entered the apartment, he told her he was leaving for Missouri. Claire asked why, and he gave her a vague answer. Claire could hardly refrain from throwing her arms around him and asking him to stay, but they returned to the pool and he visited awhile there and then left. She didn't think she would ever see him again.

One day, a nice looking gentleman came into the store needing a decorator to help him with a new office. It was quite a large job, so the boss recommended that Claire take charge of the job. The man's name was Daniel. He was a financial consultant. The job took about a year, as it was five offices, and he wanted high-quality furnishings.

While she was working on it, he asked if he and his secretary could take her to see a great stage play. Claire knew the theater was pretty formal when she accepted the offer. They said they would pick her up at her apartment. She was already dressed to the "nth" when there came a knock on the door. Claire opened it, and there stood Sig.

It had been about a year since she had seen him at the pool that day, and Claire almost couldn't recognize him he looked so bad. Instead of a spiffy, smart-looking suit, he was dressed in a sloppy pair of overalls, the kind with straps and bib. He looked like he hadn't shaved for a week. She almost felt sorry for him and was tempted to show her pity but decided against that.

Claire couldn't believe it. He said he wanted to talk to her. She said, "I'm sorry, Sig, but I'm just leaving, I have another appointment." He could see she was all dressed up.

He said, "Could I stay until you come home?"

She said, "Yes, but if you leave be sure the door is locked." When she returned home, he was not there. And the door was locked. She wondered why he came and what he was up to. In a way she felt sorry for him. Had he really gone on the skids? She never saw him again after that. He was out of her life forever, but not her thoughts.

Claire worked on that contract for Dan for over a year. She really enjoyed that one because there were no cost limitations. Claire was also taking classes to get her American Society for Interior Designing (ASID) credentials.

When Claire finished the offices for Dan, he made her an offer that took her by surprise. He asked her if she would like to open her own decorating studio and if so, where would she like it to be—he would finance the venture. As well, he had some other jobs he wanted her to handle, including his secretary's house. She thought about Dan's offer for two or three weeks and finally accepted.

After looking around, she found a place for her studio on Lido Isle, a very exclusive area of Newport Beach. Dan approved of the location. While Claire was making plans for her studio, she moved to a cute, little apartment in the nearby city of Garden Grove, close to where her friend Carol lived. (Carol was the friend she met when Claire lived near Sig in North Hollywood.) Carol was a rep for appliances at Sears, and they had kept in contact with one another.

After she was settled in, Sal paid her a visit and decided he would like to open up a styling salon in that area also. While he was looking for a location, Claire and Sal spent a lot of time together. Sal made the suggestion that they rent a condo together. Claire had not been seeing anyone else at the time. Jim had gone somewhere, so she was only seeing him when he was around and called her. Sal was still traveling to Beverly Hills, and she was back and forth from her jobs to the Furniture Mart, purchasing items she needed for Dan's job and his secretary's home in

Palos Verdes. She was also shopping for stock merchandise for their joint venture.

Claire and Sal found a place that wasn't too far from Claire's new studio. Then Sal found a location for his salon. But every night after he closed his salon, he would come home and get all dressed up and go out. He told her later that he had been eager to make more money, so he was looking for an extra job as a bartender—he was making rounds of all the bars, looking for a job. Claire didn't know if that was true or not, since she had been burned once before.

When she visited the Furniture Mart, many of the representatives wanted to take her out. One guy in particular kept asking her, so one day she accepted his offer to take her to dinner and dancing. They agreed to meet at the Stuffed Shirt, a classy restaurant. They had dinner and danced and while they were sitting there after the dance, Claire glanced up and who did she see, but Sal. She never dreamed she would see him in this place, but there he was, spiffy as ever in his new, expensive leather jacket.

The table where they were sitting was behind a post and the dance floor was crowded. Claire tried to hide, and she thought she did. Finally, when she didn't see Sal for awhile, she decided it was best to leave and go home. When she entered the apartment, he accused her immediately. He was furious. He grabbed her and lifted her up and threw her on the bed and said, "No woman of mine is going to cheat on me." Claire thought he was going to beat her. But he didn't. Sal had seen them dancing and having dinner.

Claire said, "I wasn't cheating on you, I just wanted something to do because you go out every night," to which he replied, "I go out every night to check all the bars and see if I can get a bartending job at night."

Claire asked, "Then why didn't you tell me?"

After it quieted down and she gave it more thought, Claire said, "I don't think it's a good idea for us to live together, I think I will look for another apartment."

"Well, if that is what you want, OK, but I don't want you to go. I thought we had a good thing here." Sal said.

But Claire felt that it would not work out for her, he was too possessive. So Claire found a nice studio apartment. It was a small place with kitchenette and bathroom and a Murphy bed on the wall. Claire put all of her things in that little apartment and got herself settled in.

While she was real busy getting her shop all set up and working on Dan's projects, Alan called to tell her that he and Terry were going to make her a grandma. They thought she might like to be there to see her first grandchild. So she decided to make the trip. Her little granddaughter was beautiful—Claire was so thrilled she made the trip, although it was very short.

Geri and Claire were always busy having a good time, one way or another. One night, they were out having dinner at Delaney's Sea Food, which was close to Claire's decorating studio, and they met two guys who were a lot of fun. The guys wanted them to go home with them, so Claire suggested they come to her place, which wasn't too far away. They had a few more drinks and played her stereo. They were all lying on the floor and singing with the music and having a great time. Claire knew they were safe, as she didn't open the Murphy bed! She remembers the song they kept singing: "You picked a fine time to leave me, Lucille," with Kenny Rogers. They had a hilarious time that night. Claire and Geri still laugh about it, along with all the good times they had together. Geri and Claire had a lot of fun in that little studio.

Finally, it was Christmas time, and she and Geri met another pal, Jean (she was wacky), so the three of them would get together and get into trouble when they could. She was a real character. She met a man, and they had quite an affair. He lived in one of the units in her complex. She told Geri and Claire how she would get up in the middle of the night and go to his place and have sex, then return to her unit. Claire understood that Jean had that affair for some time.

Claire finally got the store ready and had a grand opening, which was successful. It was then that she decided to move to a larger apartment and found one at a complex called the Laurel Tree in Newport Beach, very similar to the one where she lived when Sig came to see her for the last time. The complex was across the street from a grocery store called the Market Basket. From her many trips shopping there, she met one of the checkers, and her name was Bobbie. Claire and Bobbie became friends and one day, Claire invited her to her apartment. After chatting awhile, Claire found out that Bobbie was smitten by Jack, a coworker (the Deli man) at the market. He was looking for a place to live, since he was getting a divorce from his wife. Bobbie told him about the place where Claire lived, and he decided he would like to move there also. He moved into the apartment right above Claire.

Bobbie was having problems with her husband, and she decided she was going to leave him because she really had her eyes on Jack. She began to visit Claire more often so she could be close to Jack.

Claire got along well with Jack. Sometimes when she would come home from work, she would hear a thump, thump on her ceiling—it was Jack stomping the broom on the floor of his apartment to get Claire's attention. So she would go out on her balcony and look up and say, "What Jack?"

He would say, "Are you coming up here for dinner or not?"

So she would go up and have dinner with him. Sometimes Claire would cook and have Jack join her. He was affectionate with her, but he never went overboard. Finally, Claire could see Bobbie was getting jealous, so she stepped out of the picture, and then it was just Bobbie and Jack.

Bobbie finally got her divorce, and she and Jack were a twosome until they married. They bought a little house close by and had ideas of fixing it up. So they would ask Claire for her ideas, and she helped them with decorating and remodeling.

Then there was Fred. He was a rep for a wall décor company at the Furniture Mart. They became friends, and he also decided to move into the complex where Claire was living. Claire would go out with him, or they would play cards—usually penny-ante—together and occasionally with Bobbie and Jack at their little house. That was fun. Claire won enough one time to buy a new watch. When Fred and Claire would return home to their apartments, Fred always became amorous. Claire didn't want that and would make him give up on the idea.

Meanwhile, Jim (the preacher) was still in the picture. He would call or come around whenever he was in town, and she would agree to see him.

He was a very nice man, and Claire really liked him. Sometimes they would go and visit Bobbie and Jack. Also, Sal had his business going good by this time, and she would see him in his shop occasionally.

Bobbie introduced Claire to a friend who was having a problem with her husband. (It seemed that there were divorces flying around all over the place.) She was a fashion consultant—her name was Patricia, and they called her Pat. Pat had met a man called Steve. He was divorced and owned a factory making some kind of metal tool accessories, and they fell in love, so after seeing Steve for several years, Pat finally got a divorce from her husband and married Steve.

Steve had a condo in Huntington Harbor, an exclusive area close to a boat harbor, and they asked Claire to do some decorating. They were so pleased with her work that they commissioned her to do their new place in Indian Wells, an exclusive residential area, near Palm Springs. It was a very big job, and sometimes they would even furnish a car for Claire. Claire would take her friend, Geri, with her down there, and they would have a good time. Sometimes they would visit Vi who had worked for Claire years before and now managed a large thrift shop in Palm Springs. Vi had worked there for several years, ever since she moved from the little house she had when she worked for Claire.

One night, while she was still working on Pat and Steve's home, she and Geri decided to go out dancing. They went to a very popular place they had heard about called Zelda's, and while they were there, they met two guys and had a lot of fun. The guys seemed to be attracted to them. At closing time, they talked Geri and Claire into following them to the place where they were staying. They seemed to be nice men, so without hesitation and after a few drinks, Claire and Geri agreed. The place was way out in the sandy desert. The men were contracted by a company to install a new system of solar power, which was just becoming popular, and their company leased a place for them to live while they were there. They tried to entice both Claire and Geri into the bedrooms, but they didn't have any luck. Claire and Geri had a few more drinks with them and finally left. Wow! Were they daring—and lucky nothing happened! Claire and Geri know they couldn't do that today. They think about that now—how daring they were and how lucky that nothing happened.

Things were good for Claire at the shop. She was commissioned to do a job for the Finley's of Palos Verdes who owned a jewelry store. They were acquaintances of Dan's. It was not a very large job, but she did that also. From them she learned a lot about Dan that she hadn't known before.

Claire did not see her friend Rosemary very often after she moved to Newport Beach, just once in awhile they would have lunch together. One day Rosemary said, "Why don't we buy a condo together in Newport Beach—that seems to be a thriving area?"

Claire responded, "Well, I know of a condo very close to my shop, and they're really trying to sell them, so they're making them real affordable, but I don't have the down payment."

So Rosemary said, "I can get the down payment. You have to pay rent anyway, so you can make the payments and we'll split the other expenses; what do you think, Claire?" So Claire agreed and moved into the Versailles condominiums in Newport Beach, not realizing what she was taking on in the long run.

Claire decorated the condo very nicely; things seemed to be in good order; and she was content. She and Geri continued to spend a lot of time together and go places, even if they would just go for a ride on a Sunday or on a day off.

One Saturday when Claire called Geri and asked her what she would like to do that day, Geri responded, "I don't care, whatever you want do."

Claire said, "OK we'll just go for a ride around the country." They had driven many miles north when Claire said, "We're almost at Mammoth Lakes; why don't we keep going and go to Mammoth and see my son Jerry?" Geri was always a good sport and always looking for adventure, so she agreed.

When they arrived in Mammoth, Jerry was surprised to see them. He and some friends had rented a condo and they were all bunking in together. He took them out to dinner where he worked and invited them to stay the night. Claire asked, "But where will we sleep, you have no extra beds?"

Jerry said, "Don't worry, Mom, we'll arrange that." The boys all doubled up and gave the girls a bed for the night.

The next day, as they were planning to leave, Jerry said to them, "Mom, on the way back home why don't you and Geri stop at the place where I work on Sundays and have a real good dinner? I'll be working there also that night. It's off the highway a little, but not very far, and you'll enjoy it. The restaurant has a creek running through it, and they have excellent food." Always looking for something a little different, Geri and Claire agreed. They had a wonderful dinner, compliments of Jerry, then headed back to Los Angeles.

On another weekend, Geri and Claire drove southeast and came to a place that Geri recognized as the place where her ex-husband was living, so she said, "This is where Jim is now, why don't we stop and see him?" Well, they did. They met him at a saloon and spent some time with him talking and having a drink or two. They were always up to anything that was different and adventurous!

After Claire had lived at the Versailles for awhile, Jerry decided to come back to Los Angeles and moved in with her. The two of them decided to improve some things. The condo had a room that was next to the living area but not accessible from the main living area; it had its own door to the corridor. So she and Jerry decided to put a doorway between the two areas. That made an additional bedroom for the condo and a place for Jerry. They also replaced the floor in the entry with wood. That made a big improvement. Things were going pretty good for Claire at the shop and at home.

Claire had met another interior decorator, Marion, and they became friends. Marion was always living beyond her means and always had money problems, but she seemed to always have a decorating assignment. Marion and Claire would go out occasionally and sometimes on Sunday, they would just go for a ride someplace. There was a hotel in Long Beach that had dancing on Sundays. When they would go out to dinner, Jerry would generally slip Claire fifty or sixty dollars and say, "Here Mom, you girls have a good dinner and cocktails. Have a good time." He was making good wages and wanted to share.

Then Claire met a man whose name was Ray. She can't remember where she met him, but he was much older than Claire and a very nice, classy, man. He was short and always dressed nicely. He had grey hair and lived in a very exclusive apartment complex in Long Beach. He would invite Claire out to dinner at very elegant restaurants with foreign cuisines. When Claire went out with him, she was always dressed in the finest clothes.

One night he took Claire to an exclusive French restaurant in Palos Verdes and as they were enjoying their very fine dinner, a lady came over to the table and said, "Excuse my boldness, but I can't help noticing how gorgeous you look in that suit." Claire was dressed in her white leather pantsuit; the coat collar and cuffs were trimmed with white fox fur. The comment from the lady seemed to make Ray blow up with pride. Claire knew she had beautiful clothes and was very proud of them. She didn't see Ray much after that though. He was nice to her, but she couldn't reciprocate his affections.

Meanwhile, Dan's affair with his secretary was becoming noticeable; they spent more and more time together. Dan and his wife had an autistic child. Finally, he and his wife divorced, and his secretary and her husband divorced, so they were both free. (As Claire said before, the divorces were flying.) Then Dan bought a home in Palm Springs in a very posh neighborhood, very close to Liberace's home. They asked Claire to do the decorating and when they had their wedding at the home, they asked Claire to sing at their wedding. Claire sang the song "'Til." It was a significant song for them.

It was five or six months after the wedding and their house was completed when Dan decided he didn't want to put any more money into the shop. Claire thought to herself, he had gotten all the furnishings he wanted for himself, his secretary and their home in Palm Springs, so he was through.

Business started to dwindle, and Claire was on her own. Soon she couldn't handle it alone. She began selling all the stock, thinking that would clear things up. Most of the invoices were for Dan's furnishings. By this time, Claire was not having any income from the shop, and she referred all the bills to Dan. After all, he was part owner. He was not very happy about that, but Claire didn't see it any other way.

Then Rosemary decided she wasn't going to help out with the condo's extra expenses any more, so that obligation went to Claire. With the declining business in the shop, Claire didn't know how long she could hang on.

She was still friendly with Bobbie and Jack, so she often visited them in the evenings; sometimes with Jim, if he was around. Jerry was still living with Claire, and she talked to Alan by telephone. Alan urged her to move to Hawaii where he was living. Claire didn't have any idea what she would do on the island; she didn't know anyone there except her son. The last time she was there was when Alan and Terry had their first child, five years before. She was sure there would not be much there to keep her busy.

She talked to Jerry, and he thought it might be better for her to go. As he said, she could always come back if she was unhappy. She talked it over with Bobbie, and she too encouraged Claire to go. She said she would have a big, going-away, luau party for Claire and invite all of her friends.

So Claire began to make plans to leave. She decided to give the condo back to Rosemary and let her sell it. Rosemary was not very happy about that, but Claire didn't know what else to do. Then Claire sold most of her beautiful furnishings to get the money to make the move. Jerry decided he would stay in the condo until Rosemary sold the condo.

All of her friends came to Bobbie's luau party. Jim came to see her off and asked, "Why are you going over there? I'm going to miss our times together."

Claire said to him, "Jim, why don't you just go back to your wife? You know you won't find another life apart from her, and I think you still care for her."

Sometimes, when Jim and Claire were together, he would start singing that song that goes "Torn between two lovers, acting like a fool." Claire realized then that even though he had strong feelings for Claire, he was still in love with his wife.

Claire knew Rosemary wasn't very happy with her and probably neither was Dan. But she had made up her mind. Maybe she would be back and maybe not.

Sal was not at the party because she had only seen him once or twice since she left him, and Bobbie hadn't seen him either. She thought it was better that way. He was doing well with his new barber shop.

After the party, Claire went home and got into bed. As she lay there, not able to sleep, things would keep popping into her thoughts. Why couldn't she find real happiness with a man? She had worked hard and searched. But why were none of the men right for her? Well, maybe she was not destined to have a compatible partner. Maybe she should have accepted Sig as he was. No! How could she live with that? But she did love him very much, and he was always on her mind. Sometimes she would feel him caress her as he had often done, and she would wish he was there with her.

She must have finally fallen asleep, because the alarm wakened her. She had a lot of things to do today. Her friend was coming to pick up the beautiful dining room furniture, and other people were coming to get what they were buying. The next day, she had to pack all of the things she was taking with her. She had collected a lot of boxes and crates to put things in; she was going to ship them by boat. With Jerry's help, she finally completed the packing and sent everything off.

Finally, the day of her departure came, and by then she was really ready to go. She hated to leave Jerry, but he convinced her he would be OK. He had a good job, and he didn't want to leave it or his friends. Claire was not happy with him staying behind because she didn't approve of the crowd he associated with. His money was going too fast with the fast group he was chumming around with, and he was too generous with his money.

# Part Four

## HAWAII

Alan had called Claire before she left and told her he had found a cute little house for her close to where he and Terry lived. It had to have some repairs, as a hurricane had damaged the roof. When she arrived, her belongings were there ahead of her. Alan stored them at his house. Claire stayed with Alan and Terry and her granddaughter until the roof was repaired.

Alan showed Claire the little house he was able to get for her, and she thought it was really cute. She knew she could make it comfortable. Alan also had an extra car, a van he used for his plant rental services. He said, "Mom if you want something to do here, you can help me with the plants." Claire thought that would be OK for awhile. Claire loved being around her granddaughter, little Brigette.

So Claire proceeded to settle in. She stayed with Alan until the roof was completely repaired, and then she was ready to bring her things down and arrange them in the house. After she had been in the house just a few days and she had laundered some work clothes for Alan (which he wore for his night job), she decided she would go up the hill and bring down more of her things from Alan's house. She locked up her house, climbed in the van and left. Later, when Alan was on his way to his night job, he stopped at her house to change into his clean clothes.

As Claire was organizing her things at Alan's house, he phoned. He said, "Mom did you know that the screen on your back door is ripped?"

Claire said, "No I never noticed."

"Well, there's a big rip in it like someone cut it."

Immediately Claire became frightened, remembering her jewelry, which she had put away. In an excited voice she yelled, "See if my diamond rings and jewelry are still there in the dresser drawer." He left the phone for a moment.

When he came back on the line, he said, "Mom I don't see any jewelry or diamond rings."

Claire's heart dropped to the floor. She cherished the rings that Sig had given her and the gold chains and ring Jerry had given her. She had had diamonds mounted into Jerry's ring. She immediately jumped into the van and made her way down to the little house.

Oh! This was a very bad day. Even though Alan always said, "You don't need to lock your house here, Mom, no one ever bothers you." She had locked everything up anyway. Claire was absolutely devastated. Why did this happen to her? That night and many nights after, she cried herself to sleep; she was not to get that off her mind for a long time. She felt empty without her jewelry.

After contacting the police department and filing a burglary report, Claire drew up pictures of every piece she had lost, and she contacted all the jewelry stores in the state. No one had received anything like her pieces. The police told her that the thieves melt all the gold down and ship it out of the state. She still kept on praying she would get them back.

After a few weeks on the Island , Claire decided she would like to have some chickens, so Alan went into town and brought back a couple of dozen baby chicks, and Claire started to raise chickens and fix up the yard.

There were some very good banana plants on the property, and about a year after she was in the house, Claire and Alan decided one day to move them and make a regular banana garden. Alan was digging them up and Claire was replanting them. All of a sudden Alan yelled out to Claire in a very frightened voice, "Mom, come here, come here, and don't be upset. Take it easy, come here."

Claire thought he had found a dead body or something. She ran to Alan, and he held out his hand. Claire saw a slimy bunch of something in his hand, but she couldn't tell what it was.

Alan said, "I think these are yours, Mom." Claire looked again and saw two large rings. She exclaimed, "Alan, those are my rings; where did you find them?"

He replied, "I was just digging here and they came up. I thought they were tops for cans at first, then I thought they were play rings for Brigette. Finally, I realized what they were."

Claire was so happy she was crying. She couldn't believe that one whole year had passed and they were lying out there in that dirt all that time. Her prayers were answered.

Ever since she had arrived on Kauai, Alan had been encouraging Claire to take the real estate exam. He had taken his a few years before and got his license (which he let expire). He would say, "Mom, get your license. You'd do well, as real estate sales are up now." Claire checked, and there had been a class on the island, but nothing was being offered now.

Time went on, and Claire was helping Alan with his plant service. A few of Alan's friends heard that his mother had come to Kauai to live, that she was an interior decorator, and that she had had a shop in California. It was not long before she received a few requests to do some decorating for them. It was difficult because there wasn't a source for materials or supplies on the island.

Several people suggested that Claire start a class in interior decorating. She ran this through her mind awhile and finally decided to go to the local college and see if they had a class. They didn't, but they were interested in having one. So Claire advertised and spread the word and received quite a few interested students. Then she conducted her class, the first one on the island. She had sales people from furniture stores, daughters of grocery store owners, housewives—all kinds of ladies enrolled. Her class was very well received, but it only lasted one semester, as many couldn't afford it on an ongoing basis.

Then one day, out of the blue, Claire received a call from Esther's daughter, Elaine. She asked if Claire could find it in her heart to forgive her mother for the treatment she gave Claire when she was growing up. Claire responded by saying that she could forgive her but, didn't think she could ever forget. Claire wondered later why Elaine would call to get that answer. Was her mother sick and going to pass on or what? Claire decided then that that book was closed, and she didn't want to think about it anymore.

By this time, Claire decided to pursue the real estate business. She checked into the classes again and found that although there were none on Kauai, she could take a correspondence course from Oahu, so she applied and started the course. It was a much slower process by mail.

One day, Terry's mother asked her if she would like to go on a home tour to see some of the elite homes on the island and how they were decorated. Claire readily accepted. While they were looking around one of the homes, Claire met a very nice lady named Reenie. She asked Claire if she worked on the island, and Claire explained that she helped her son with the plant service. Then she invited Claire to work in the jewelry store where she worked. We need someone like you," she said. "I know you'd be good." Claire thought about all the jewelry she owned, but had never considered selling any.

Reenie continued, "Oh, I know it wouldn't take you long to learn all about it, so come on by and talk to the owner."

So in a few days, Claire got up enough nerve to go and meet the owners. The name of the store was, Wales Fine Jewelers. She liked them and they seemed to like her, so they hired her. Claire worked there for a year or more. When they decided to sell the store, the new people who bought it, Grande Gems, requested that Claire stay on and work for them. She did for about a year longer. She was doing very well and meeting people.

Claire was still living in the cute little house, fixing it up every chance she got. One day, a local man approached Claire in the store. He said he was attracted to her right away, and after coming in several times, he asked if she would go to lunch with him. He was a Filipino man who had lived on the island for many years. She accepted his lunch invitation. After that, he continued to come around, asking her to go out with him again. But she couldn't see anything in common, so she refused his invitations.

Alan got word that his dad had passed away, and he was making preparations to go back for the funeral. Claire said to him, "You'll see your brother; why don't you convince him to come back here with you?" Alan said he would see what he could do. And when he returned, Jerry was with him. Claire was happy. Jerry moved in with Claire, and it wasn't long before he found employment. He made a few job changes after that and finally went to work for a friend of Alan's where he's been working ever since, doing very well.

Claire had visits from a few of her California friends. Marion came and so did Bobbie and Jack. Vi and her friend came also, and Claire accommodated all of them. Claire had fun showing them the beauty of the island.

One day, a lady came into the store looking for a piece of jewelry, and she and Claire had a conversation. She told Claire she had a real estate office in the town of Lihue, on the island. She also said she knew Claire's son, Alan, when he had his real estate license. Her name was Laverne, and her office was called Maile Properties.

After a few visits, Laverne began to encourage Claire to get her license and work for her as a sales agent. Claire continued to study for the real estate exam while she worked in the jewelry store, and after about a year, she was finally ready. When Laverne heard that she got her license, she insisted Claire go to work for her.

Claire said, "But I have this job in the store, and I'm doing very well, so how can I work for you?"

Laverne said, "You can still work for me. Since you're working the late shift at the jewelry store, from three to ten p.m., you can work in my office, from nine a.m. until two p.m. So Claire went to work as a real estate agent for Maile Properties.

Claire made a lot of friends from both Kauai and the mainland through her real estate transactions and was doing better than she'd hoped.

Her broker at the office was always trying to fix Claire up with some of the gentlemen on the island, but Claire couldn't see herself with any of them. One day she said to Claire, "Hey, Claire, I know this man who would be perfect for you. His wife has recently left him, and he's devastated and is planning a divorce. He's from the mainland and he's very good looking—just the type of man you would go for. He has a great personality, and is a lot of fun. He's from Oregon and has retired in Kauai. He has a lot of property here. I know he's lonely and would like someone as a companion. "I'm trying to persuade him to come to work for me here at the office. He has his license with another office, but he's not very happy there."

Claire grinned and said, "Well, when you get him here I guess I'll meet him."

"He'll come in here one of these days," said Laverne

Claire was at her desk working on a deal one morning when this tall, good-looking man walked in. Laverne immediately introduced him to all of the agents and said he would be a new agent with them. Claire knew immediately who he was. His name was Bob Gilbert. Laverne assigned a box to him in the file room where he could pick up his correspondence. He looked it over and said goodbye and left.

A few days later, an office meeting was planned at the local bank. Bob came into the office a little early, and Claire was in the file room. She greeted him and said, "I understand you're going to be joining us."

He nodded and after a minute, he said to her "Are you going to our office meeting this morning? Would you like to ride with me? There's no sense taking two cars." Claire accepted his offer.

After that day, Bob came into the office regularly. The other agents told Bob that Claire had been an interior decorator and had her ASID credentials. He teased Claire about that, asking if she was a member of ACID. She didn't think, at that time that he even knew what ASID stood for.

One morning when he came into the office, he said he had just picked up some paintings, which he had framed, and he wanted to know if Claire would give him some direction to hang them.

Claire said she would, but she needed him to describe the size and height of the wall and where they would be going in reference to the windows, etc. Finally he asked, "Can you come to my house and help me?"

Claire said, "Yes, I can stop on my way home."

Bob being considerate, replied, "Don't you think that will be out of your way?"

Claire said, "No, I can stop by tomorrow after I leave the office." So, he agreed and said he would look forward to seeing her there.

The next day, Claire left the office early and using his directions, went to his home. As she drew near, she recognized his property as one she had watched several years earlier.

When she had visited Alan before she even moved to Kauai, she was attracted to this very pretty piece of property, and at that time, she noticed a man planting small trees in immaculate rows. No matter how you would look at them, they were perfectly straight. She didn't know why, but she was intrigued by the neatness, and every time she would drive by, she noticed that.

This day, as she approached the gate, she could see the trees were mature and still perfectly placed. Who was this man? Could this be the same property that attracted her years ago? The gate was open, so she drove directly onto the property up to the large home. She parked the car and started to walk toward the house when she saw Bob near the back of the house. He was beckoning her to come to the back patio.

Claire noticed he was wearing shorts, and he had very attractive legs for a man. Why was she attracted to his legs? She had never been attracted to a man's legs before. She decided she could be very attracted to all of him. Claire noticed that he was drinking some kind of a cocktail, and he asked if she would join him.

Claire replied, "No thanks, I'll just take a glass of water, please." Bob went into the house and returned with the glass of water. (Later in their relationship, he told her he was thinking, what kind of girl is this who won't take a cocktail?)

He led her into the living room and pointed out where he would like the pictures to go. Claire gave him good directions, and he seemed to appreciate them. After some small talk, he said he'd like to take her out to dinner one night. He asked if she would go. She accepted, but explained that she would need to make it when she had her night off from the jewelry store, because she worked until nine-thirty or ten. So they made it on her night off. As she talked to him, she began to like him very much. He seemed to be well educated, more than some she had met on the island, and seemed to have more class.

On their first date, Bob took Claire to a restaurant called the Bull Shed.

They talked and became more acquainted. She can't remember what she ate, but she can tell you exactly where they were seated—by the window where they could watch the ocean waves. It seemed as if the waves were going to come right in the window. As they were leaving, Bob ask Claire if she liked to dance, and she answered, "Oh, yes."

He asked her if she had ever gone to the Cocoa Palms, and she replied, "I've been there for brunch a couple of times but never to dance."

So he took her to the ballroom at the Cocoa Palms, and they danced for a couple of hours to the music of Larry Rivera, a well known, local songwriter and musician. As they danced, Claire was sure that Bob was a little embarrassed because he was over a foot taller than Claire. But that didn't stop him from holding her real close.

They returned to his house where Claire was to pick up her car, and he said to Claire, "I'd like to see you again if that's agreeable with you."

Claire replied, "Of course."

The next time he came into the office, he approached Claire and asked, "What are you doing Sunday? I'd like to have you come to my house, and I'll make breakfast."

Claire replied, "That would be nice, but I go to church in the morning."

"Well that's OK. What time do you get out of church? I can make brunch then." With that they set a time.

When Claire arrived for the breakfast, Bob had it all set up on the patio with a Bloody Mary to start out. From then on he wanted to see her every night. Needless to say, Claire was very pleased, as they seemed to be very compatible.

Because she was working nights, Bob sometimes prepared a basket dinner and brought it down to the jewelry store. When she locked up, they went to the nearby beach and set up the beach chairs he brought with him; then he poured the martinis, and they drank them before enjoying the picnic that he had prepared. When Claire saw him enter the store, her heart started pounding, and she became all excited. Claire couldn't imagine anyone being that thoughtful. He was so sweet to her.

On the nights that Claire had off, Bob prepared dinner at his home and she joined him there. When she went to his place for dinner, he would have it set up on the glass game table in the living room and have the stereo playing beautiful music. The second time she came to dinner they were sitting there talking after dinner. Bob got up, came over to Claire, and put his arms around her. He lifted her up and pulled her down on the floor with him and embraced her lovingly.

"Bob, what are you doing?" she asked.

"I want you to be beside me, and I want to hug and kiss you." As the music became mellower, he became more loving and Claire was taking in every drop of it. She knew she could really love this man. He was what she had always hoped for—sweet, gentle and considerate.

One day, the real estate office was having an office party at a local Chinese restaurant. The broker said to Bob, "Of course you must come too."

When Bob heard that, he said to Claire, "You'll be going with me to the party won't you?"

Claire accepted his invitation. She was thrilled he wanted her close to him. When Claire arrived at his house, she was dressed in an off-white rayon crepe Palazzo suit, and according to Bob, she looked lovely. Bob looked very handsome in his white trousers and Hawaiian shirt. He was so handsome! She didn't know he was going to wear white, and he didn't have any idea what she would be wearing. They made a very handsome couple. He stayed close to Claire all evening, and they had a lovely time. Everyone insisted they have their picture taken together, which they did.

When the party broke up, they left and headed for Bob's house where Claire had left her car. On the way, they talked about their respective lives. Bob described his marital woes, which were quite shocking to Claire.

Prior to retiring, Bob had owned a very large construction business in Oregon—he built shopping centers, bridges, highways, etc. He told Claire how he was involved with a group called SCORE, which stood for Successful Corp of Retired Executives (something to that effect). It was a group of executives and owners of large businesses who were requested by the government to instruct people who wanted to go into business for themselves, and hold seminars for that purpose. SCORE entailed a lot of traveling for him, as his territory was the South Pacific, from San Francisco, west.

After one such a trip to the South Pacific, when he was still with his wife, he was to go to a meeting at his headquarters in San Francisco, then later meet her in Oregon. In the meantime, without him knowing, she made arrangements to have someone move everything out of their home in Hawaii while he was gone. She was not where they were to meet on the mainland. He checked every place he thought she might be, with no luck. When he walked into their home in Hawaii, the house was bare. To say the least, the poor man was devastated.

As Bob finished his story and they approached his house, he turned to Claire and asked if she would come in. Claire said, "Yes, for a little while."

He mixed drinks for both of them. Then he put his arms around her and said, "Claire I'd like you to stay with me tonight, and if you're uneasy about it, you can stay in the guest room."

Claire replied, "I can't do that, Bob. I'm not prepared, and I'd need to let my son, Jerry, know." Jerry was still living with Claire at her little house.

"Will you make arrangements to stay with me tomorrow night?" It was as if he didn't want to be alone.

Claire thought awhile and answered, "Yes, I'll tell Jerry and bring the things I'll need for work." Her heart began to flutter. Bob still had not made love to her. Considering all his affections, she had begun to think that maybe something was wrong. She was beginning to yearn for more than hugging and kissing.

Claire did stay the next two nights in the guest room. Bob made up a sign and hung it on the front door as a joke. It read, "Robert's Over-Nighter."

Bob asked her if Claire would consider going away with him, not far, "Just somewhere where we can be alone."

Claire agreed, "But it will need to be after July fourth, as my grandson's first birthday party is on the fourth. Bob said he would figure out where they were going and let her know.

He said he wanted to make mad love to her, but he preferred that it wasn't on that island where everyone knew him. He must have thought the word would get around the island, and he would be embarrassed. Claire didn't know why, but whatever his idea was, they took off for Hilo on the fifth of July. On the plane, he told her he had reserved a room at the Huki Lau Hotel and wanted to know her favorite food. She told him it was lobster. He said he knew just the place. On the way to the hotel Bob said, "We'll stop at a liquor store and pick up something to have at the hotel." So they did.

When they got to the hotel, they were both laden down with luggage and packages. Claire carried the refreshments, and just as Bob opened the door, down went the bottle of vodka with a crash on the threshold. It was so loud that all the other guests opened their doors to see what happened. Needless to say, Bob and Claire were both embarrassed.

Bob said to Claire, "Don't worry, Honey, we'll get this cleaned up and I'll go and get another one." And he did.

When he returned, they had a couple of cocktails. Then Bob said, "Now we're going for that lobster."

The name of the restaurant was called Rosie's Seafood. Bob ordered martinis and lobster dinners for both. They sat and talked for awhile. Since Claire hadn't had a martini for a long time, they began to have an effect on her and she couldn't finish her lobster. She told Bob they had better leave while she could walk out on her own.

When they got to the hotel, Bob had to help her undress, and she just flopped in bed. She doesn't know how long she was asleep, but Bob awakened her making love to her. When she realized what he was doing, she had the strongest urge to return his love, so she did. That was the first time he had really come to her, and it was great. She knew then that he had been holding back for some reason, and it wasn't physical. He said he hadn't made love for a long time, and that it was the best.

After a few weeks of Claire staying with Bob at his house, he asked her to move in with him, as he wanted her there all the time. Claire told Jerry of Bob's invitation, and Jerry said, "If that's what you want Mom, it's OK with me."

Claire finally moved in with Bob permanently; it just seemed to be the thing to do for both of them.

At night, when Bob would embrace her, he would say, "Gotcha, Honey. Why didn't we meet thirty-five years ago? We missed a lot of fun. We probably would have had a lot of kids because we were made for each other."

One night after she came in from work, Bob said to Claire," Honey, how would you like it if I drew a nice bath for you? You could take a nice warm bubble bath before dinner."

"That sounds delicious," She replied.

As she was in the bath, submerged in lots of bubbles, in walked Bob, handing her a martini. Then, before she knew it, he had a camera and snapped her picture. He loved to surprise her like that.

The more they were together, the more they were in love. This went on for months. They discussed marriage, but Bob was afraid to take another chance—since his last one was such a disappointment. He would never agree to getting married. But Claire never stopped asking.

The people who owned the jewelry store decided they would close that store and open one on Maui, so Claire didn't work for them any longer. Bob was happy about that because he liked her being at home in the evenings.

One day a client walked into the real estate office, and Claire approached him to see if she could help him. He introduced himself as Ed Cates and said he was looking for a piece of commercial property as an investment. Claire did some searching and showed him several, but they were not exactly to his liking. Then she found a great piece of property in town across from the mall, and she checked it out. The price was very high, in the millions, but he really liked the site. The property included a large heritage home, which Ed thought could be converted to a beautiful restaurant. It had a beautiful curved staircase in the entry.

The next time he came to the island, he brought his wife with him, and Claire and Bob had them to their house for cocktails. They all became friends. Then Ed decided he wanted to put a large "earnest money" deposit on the property, so Claire wrote up the offer. But when the offer was presented to the seller, it turned out that he had decided to donate the property to his wife's church.

Ed was devastated. They could never find anything else as appropriate as that. But Ed and Barbara and Claire and Bob remained friends after that.

Ed said to them, "If you folks ever come our way, be sure and plan to visit us." Bob thanked them for the invitation, but didn't have any idea when they would be going that way.

Sometimes on a weekend, Bob made plans for both of them to go camping in the mountains. He rented a log cabin and had the car all loaded with supplies and wood for the fireplace when she got home from work. They would have a glorious time there, making love by the fire place.

The cabin was cute, but it had very high ceilings with just a light bulb for a chandelier. This made the cabin seem so bare. Finally, Claire said, "Bob remind me when we come again to bring a hanging lamp. I can't stand that light in the ceiling, and I'd like to have something over the table when we have dinner."

Bob said to Claire, "Do you want a lamp over the table?"

Claire replied, "Yes, I would." With that, Bob went outside, and in a few minutes came back with a hanging lamp. It was made from a coffee can and an extension cord, and he hung it over the little table. He was so ingenious with so many things. Claire threw her arms around him and kissed him. She loved him doing things like that.

That night Bob said to Claire, "Honey I think I'm going to move the bed into the living room in front of the fire, and we'll be cozy and warm all night."

Claire said, "That sounds great." So together they moved it. They curled up in bed with Claire in Bob's arms, and he squeezed her to him and said, as he did many times, "Gotcha, Honey." Soon they were making love more intently than the fire in the fireplace. Then she cuddled in Bob's arms and as they watched the embers in the fireplace, they both fell asleep.

One day, Claire received a phone call from Al's half-sister, Della, who was still living in California. She said her husband was dying and asked if Claire would come and be with her to help her through the trauma. Claire was thinking about what she should do when Bob spoke up and said, "Honey, if you think you should go, you go, and I'll hold down the fort. If Della doesn't want to stay there alone after he goes, she can come to Hawaii and build a house on the other side of our property." Bob knew that Claire and Della had a close relationship. Claire went and stayed until Della's husband passed on. She told Della what Bob had offered, and Della said she would consider that offer.

Claire and Bob always spent holidays together, along with Claire's boys, who seemed to like Bob. One holiday, they were all in the kitchen talking when Bob spoke up. He said, "Your mom and I are thinking about getting married; what do you boys think about that?"

Claire was shocked because Bob had never committed to marrying her, even though she persisted on the subject. Jerry was taken aback a little. All Alan said was, "Gee, I'll have to buy some new shoes (since everyone on the islands wore flip-flops). They all laughed. Both agreed it was a good idea.

Bob said, "Don't worry about shoes. I don't think we'll be married on the island; we'll probably go somewhere else, just the two of us." Alan thought that was a great plan, especially since he wasn't for crowds or parties. After all, Claire and Bob had been living together for over three years at this point, and Bob's divorce was final.

Afterward, Claire asked Bob, "What were you thinking? That was a surprise."

He replied, "Well we might as well; we're practically married now. But I don't want to get married on this island." So Claire suggested they go to Las Vegas to marry; and she could have her friend, Carol, make the arrangements since Carol was living in Las Vegas.

Claire was so happy and set the date—January eleventh, nineteen ninety-nine, because she believed that the number one was a lucky number for her. Bob agreed to the date.

When the day came for them to leave for Vegas, Claire had everything prepared, including all the Hawaiian leis and flowers and her new, beautiful off-white suit with shoes to match, which she had purchased for the occasion. She was walking on air, she was so happy. When she told her friend, Geri, about the decision, Geri said she would be there—she wouldn't miss it for the world for after all, Claire was her best friend.

The wedding ceremony was lovely. Carol and her husband, Ken, stood up for them, and of course Geri was the bridesmaid. Bob insisted they play the Hawaiian wedding song during the ceremony. Claire noticed that Bob had tears in his eyes when they spoke the vows.

After the ceremony, Bob took the group out to dinner. What a sweetheart he was! He really was her darling. He was the only one in her life who she ever addressed as "Darling." That was the night of all nights. Bob made love to her like she had never experienced before. It felt like he didn't want to let her go.

The next day, Claire received a little surprise. She and Bob were walking past one of the casinos and who did they run into but Fred, who Claire dated when she lived at the Laurel Tree apartments. It had been a long time. Claire introduced Bob, Fred congratulated them, and they walked on.

A few weeks later, Bob was to go to Samoa for his SCORE group, and he invited her to go with him. Claire was delighted. They went for a week, and Claire considered that to be a honey moon. She found the experience very interesting.

In June of that year (Claire was still working in real estate), Bob asked

Claire if she would like to go to Australia and she answered, "Of course, when?"

He said, "Well, I found a good trip for August, and if you'd like to go I'll make the arrangements." Bob made all the arrangements, and it was like a second honeymoon.

Before they left Hawaii, Bob said to Claire, "You pick the tour you think you'd like, and I'll pick one that interests me." So he selected the river cruise tour, and Claire selected the airplane cruise. When they arrived, the river cruse had been cancelled, so they both settled for the airplane tour. Bob was happy that they didn't make the river tour as he was thrilled with the air tour.

What a wonderful trip that was! Bob had planned for everything. He rented an apartment in Sydney, and that was to be their base. Then he made reservations for an air tour, which would take them all over Australia for six days and five nights.

The tour began in Sydney. The first day, they visited Broken Hill for an authentic outback sheep shearing and enjoyed an Aussie lunch of barbecued lamb; then to Cooper Pedy. Then they visited the opal mines and stayed one night in a fabulous underground hotel, which was furnished lavishly; then to Ayers Rock for one night in a luxurious hotel. The next stop was Alice Springs for one night, then to Cairns for a glass-bottom boat tour; then to the Great Barrier Reef overnight; then back toward Sydney and the apartment.

After the Barrier Reef, Bob said to Claire, "What do you say we leave the tour, rent a car and drive around, see the country up here and drive back to Sydney?"

Claire said, "That sounds fine with me, do you think you can stay on the correct side of the road?"

Bob laughed and replied, "I think I can manage OK." So they drove back to Sydney from Queensland, and he only got on the wrong side once. The whole excursion was first-class.

The balance of the two weeks was spent in Sydney, and they had a glorious time. Bob got to see a lot of things he wanted to see, like the museum in Darling Harbor. Bob got up each morning and walked down to the little store on the corner. It was actually a house, which the owners had made into a small store where you could buy bread, milk, bakery items, and a few other things. He bought breakfast rolls and had coffee ready for Claire when she awoke. They had a leisurely breakfast together before going out to see the sights. They did a great deal of walking. Then it was back home and back to work for Claire; and time to be alone with her darling Bob again.

When they returned home, she began to redecorate some of the house. She redid the master bedroom because it wasn't the way she liked it. It had never been decorated. Bob bought her a new sewing machine with a cabinet and all the attachments. She made new draperies and a bedspread and recovered the bench with coordinated materials. It turned out beautifully. She redecorated the guest room so it would look nice if Della came to visit. And they bought new appliances for the kitchen and redid the countertops with ceramic tile that had custom designed patterned tiles here and there. It looked very pretty. Bob was very pleased; he couldn't believe what a difference it made.

It was around this time that Claire decided to move to another real estate office—Summers Realty—which was closer to home. She could get home earlier and help her darling pick nuts in the orchard—she thought of this as her exercise. Bob always visited her wherever she was working.

In July of the following year, Claire received a letter from Della who said she was thinking seriously about Bob's offer to let her build a house on his property. She was going to plan a trip to Hawaii and would talk it over with them.

In August of that year (nineteen ninety-two), Della made definite plans to visit Bob and Claire. She arrived a few weeks later in early September when the weather was still beautiful. Bob and Claire explained to her where the house could be on their property and how they would cut off a small parcel of their nut orchard to make room. She was getting excited about the prospect. She wouldn't feel alone, being near her nieces and nephews and Claire (whom she and her husband always regarded as part of her family). Every day they talked about what she would like in the house.

They all went up to the mountains for a couple of days, and she really enjoyed the trip, as well as Bob's humor.

On September ninth, Bob, Claire and Della were on the patio discussing everything from the type of house Della would like to the harvest of the macadamia nuts Bob hoped he was going to have that year. Suddenly, they all noticed that the air had become very still.

Bob said, "We better listen to the news regarding Hurricane Iniki, which is lurking out in the ocean. They say it's not moving fast, and if it stays on the same course, it will miss us." So all evening they listened to the weather station, checking on the hurricane. When they retired that evening, the latest news broadcast announced that it was heading west and would probably miss the island of Kauai.

Bob awoke very early the next morning to get the news, and when Claire and Della awoke, Bob said, "I better go down to Tool Master and see if they've completed the repair on our big generator. We may need it." (Bob had it there for a month now as they always took it in to have it checked when hurricane season was approaching.) "If it isn't ready yet, I'll bring it back and fix it myself." By then the news was that the hurricane had veered north and picked up speed. This made Della and Claire very nervous.

Before Bob left, they all got busy and filled the bathtubs and everything they could find that would hold water and made lots of ice. Bob had remarked that maybe it would be a good idea for them to make a big pot of stew, something that would last them a couple of days because they might not have anything to cook with, like a stove or microwave oven. Then he left to get the generator. When he returned, he had the generator, but it had not been repaired.

Claire and Della headed for the market to buy food for the big stew and anything they thought they might need, such as masking tape for the windows—they had run out of that. They checked all over, but everyone was sold out of it. The little town of Kapaa was absolute bedlam, as Claire was sure every part of the island was by now.

On the way back to the house, Claire turned the car radio on to check the latest news, and they heard the mayor speaking, giving everyone a warning; it was about nine-thirty in the morning. The mayor's voice was strong and clear. She ordered all the businesses closed and everyone off the streets, even police and firemen, by ten thirty. She announced that the storm was expected to hit land at approximately one in the afternoon. She directed people who were not secure to head for the disaster shelters, and she gave their locations. After hearing all of that, Claire's skin was crawling, and she was sure Della was shaking in her shoes. On the way home from the market, it started to rain slightly.

When they arrived back at the house, Claire and Della immediately put on the meat to prepare the stew. Bob was scurrying around trying to get everything ready, making sure the generator was working and that they had plenty of propane for the barbecue.

Suddenly, the radio station went off. They could feel the wind pick up velocity. It must have been about fifty or sixty miles an hour at that time. They had just put the potatoes and vegetables into the stew when the electricity went off. Since their range had solid elements, they stayed hot longer, so the potatoes did get done.

By then it was nearing one o'clock. The wind was getting stronger, and Claire and Della were getting very scared. Bob was doing everything he could to make them comfortable. Claire knew then why she loved Bob so much—he was so sweet and thoughtful.

Della and Claire were sitting in the living room—Bob had pushed all the furniture to the front end so it wouldn't get damaged if the windows broke. They could see the roof on the patio room going up and down with the wind. Della remarked, "That roof is going to go any time now." (It survived the storm, but was pretty bent.)

Bob came into the house, and he pointed out the large, thirty-foot avocado tree near the house. It was trying to resist the wind, and they could see the huge root ball moving up and down out of the ground. And the ground was raising and lowering with it. In a few minutes, it couldn't resist any longer and tore out of the ground. They watched it roll with the wind and were hoping it wouldn't crash into the window of the house. It finally blew over to the neighbor's property. The wind kept on picking up speed.

Bob said to Claire, "I think we had better get into the doorway of our laundry closet." So he put two bar stools in there for Claire and Della to sit on and told them to stay there. From that angle, they could see the large kitchen window bulging in and out. The wind was so strong that it looked like a sheet of frosted glass flying across the property, along with parts of buildings. All Della and Claire could do was cling to each other, praying that it would stop.

Bob was close to the window, watching, and it made Claire nervous. She kept yelling at him to get away from the window and stand by them. She was so afraid something would fly through the window, and he would be hurt.

All of a sudden, they heard a loud crashing of glass, and Bob ran toward his office, with Claire and Della following. One of the jalousie windows had blown out, Bob grabbed the top part of Claire's drafting table to put up at the window, but the wind was so strong he couldn't. Claire helped him, and together they managed to push his steel desk up to hold the drafting board in place. Claire ran to find something to put all the broken glass in, and they all started to clean it up.

Just as they were walking out of the room, the door blew shut behind them and in a split second came this horrible explosion-like crash. Bob grabbed Claire and Della and pushed them into the guest bathroom nearby. They all felt glass hitting them, but didn't look to see how bad it was. Later, they saw lots of cuts and blood. They discovered afterward that a large four-by-four beam from the house next door had blown through the wall of Bob's office, blowing out the windows and caused the explosive sound.

Della and Claire stayed in the guest bathroom for nearly four hours. Bob kept going in and out to see what was happening with the water lines, but finally discovered they were gone. Della and Claire could hear all kinds of crashing noises, and something kept banging against the wall of the bathroom where they stood. They both prayed over and over,

"God, please let this room hold out." They didn't try to look outside, even though they wanted to see what was happening.

Claire finally looked out and saw that the door to Bob's office had blown off and was banging against the outside wall of the bathroom. That was the banging noise they were hearing. Bob came in and told them that the roof was gone, and then the living room wall was gone, and so on. Her poor, sweet darling Bob had to watch his beautiful home blow away.

By this time, the day was getting into the evening hours. Claire does not remember looking at her watch, but the wind seemed to be subsiding a little. Claire said to Della, "Thank God! Do you suppose it's over?" and they peeked out the door.

At that time, Bob joined them and informed them that it was the "eye" of the storm, and the second half would be coming soon. In unison they both cried, "Oh, no!"

When they came out of the bathroom to look around at the damage, they couldn't believe their eyes. The entire house seemed to be gone. All that remained was the kitchen, guest bathroom, hallway, and part of the stairs to the second floor. They had no idea of the extent of the damage upstairs as yet. They could see the kitchen walls had moved, and the ceiling had a large crack in it, and the new tile counters had cracked away from the walls. The dining room was a lake about a foot deep as the roof was gone and the rain just poured in.

Bob herded them back into the laundry closet to ride out the second half of the storm, which was coming now. Della and Claire just clung to each other and prayed some more. Claire kept worrying about Bob because he would go in and out in the storm to see what the damage was, and Claire feared he would get hurt. Claire's heart went out to him as he was seeing the years of hard work he had put into this house and orchard being totally blown away.

Claire was also thinking of her children and grand children. Were they OK? She feared their little, single-wall house would not hold up under this terrible wind. Also they were in the midst of building a new house, and it was not complete. The new house was very close to where Claire and Bob lived. While it was being built, they were renting a little house, which was located down the hill in the town of Kapaa.

From the laundry closet, Claire and Della could see out the kitchen window at all the debris flying by again, as it did during the first half. By this time, they could see all of the trees in the orchards were horizontal, and they could hear more crashing noises. It was an eerie feeling, like the whole world was gone—all but this terrible wind; it was like having your ears plugged, but you could still hear the roar of the train.

In a short time, they could feel the storm begin to subside again. They asked Bob, "Is it going to come back again?"

Bob replied, "I don't think so, we'll just have rain and some wind." It finally got down to a strong gale and slowly subsided.

Together, they began to take an account of all of the damage. They could see from the downstairs that the master bedroom was mostly gone. So they climbed the broken stairs to the upstairs bedrooms and could see all the rooms were gone, except for a couple of walls, and most all of the furniture had blown away. The clothing in the dressers had blown out of the drawers and the rain had soaked all of their clothing in the dressing room, and all of the linens in the linen closet, because the door had blown off. They realized then that the storm had let up. Claire doesn't remember if they had the stew that night or not, it may have blown off the range.

It was dark by this time, and they began to discuss how they were going to sleep that night as everything was gone or damaged, and they were all exhausted. The master bedroom was upstairs, and the living room was downstairs and had a very high ceiling and a window up high on one wall into the master bedroom. You could look through that window from the bedroom into the living room downstairs. That wall was gone, but to get to the master bedroom, you could go up through that window.

Bob found a box spring that hadn't blown away, under a bunch of rubble. He went up and lowered it down through that window and let it slide down on some rafters that were sort of propped there, and he lowered it down to Claire. He also lowered down a metal frame to put it on.

The mattress had blown about a mile away and landed on some people's roof.

Claire said, "Oh! Good, Bob, we can sleep on that at least, and we can put it up in the dining room."

Then Bob said, "We can't sleep on that, it's soaked with water."

Claire thought a minute, and said, "We'll sleep on that because I'll fix it so we can. I'll just put this plastic tarp that we have here on the box spring under the bedding and also a piece of plastic on the top of our bedding, to keep the rain off and keep the bedding dry.

The floor was a lake, about five or ten inches deep with lots of broken glass, and while Claire was trying to get the bed ready, she walked on a piece of glass and sliced her big toe wide open. She couldn't get it to stop bleeding. Of course, they had no bandages or first-aid available, so she found a towel and wrapped it around her foot. That didn't do much good because she had to wade in the water. Sweet Bob was so upset and worried about her toe, he went all over to find some bandages.

She finally completed making the bed for them, in this "lake," and they all climbed in fully dressed. There wasn't much room in the bed for the three of them. Bob was holding on to Claire as if he was afraid of losing her.

Della made the remark that she couldn't remember ever climbing into bed fully clothed. They were so exhausted they could care less. Sleeping between two pieces of plastic was like three people in a sauna. Needless to say, they didn't sleep all night. Their adrenalin had risen so high, they couldn't come down. Bob finally got up at two or three o'clock and started roaming around, checking out the damage and seeing if the water pipes were broken. He discovered they were. Claire was so nervous about Bob roaming around outside in the storm.

In the morning, Della and Claire got up and walked through the "lake" around the bed to make the inspection to see if anything was left. It seemed that the only room in the house that wasn't touched on the inside was the guest bathroom where they huddled during the storm. The guest room where Della stayed was absolutely demolished, and everything had blown out, including Claire's new sewing machine and the furniture. All of the walls were gone. Della felt very weird seeing the room where she stayed completely gone.

Bob was busy trying to repair the broken water pipe so they could have water. Of course, they wouldn't be able to drink it, but they'd be able to flush the toilets

Della and Claire decided to walk out to the street, which was about six hundred feet to the front gate to see how everyone else had managed. The sight they saw was horrible. Telephone and electric poles and lines and trees all over the road, and people were walking around in a traumatic daze.

Claire met one man carrying a very small child. And he was trying to tell her about his house blowing apart, and he started crying and said all he could do was cling to the child as his roof blew off. Another lady came by on a bicycle looking for someone who had medical experience to help her husband who was cut severely by flying glass—she thought he may have severed a tendon. Then they met a lady Claire knew, who was trying to drive her car through the rubble in the street, she wanted to find her horse, but of course she couldn't get more than a hundred feet.

She said, "Hi, Claire, how did you make out?" Claire told her they had lost their house completely and she started to cry and said she had also, but she wanted to make sure her horse was OK.

Claire still didn't hear anything from her children, and she was getting more upset. Jerry was on another island, so she thought that he was OK. But she was sure Alan and Terry and the children would try to reach her if they were alright, but still they had no word.

Della and Claire came back to the house and proceeded to pick things up and hang them to dry out. Then Bob decided he was going to put some tarps on the roof of the garage, which had a large hole in it where the roof blew off. He climbed up and was trying to spread the tarp, but he was having a hard time with the strong wind. Claire felt sorry for him. She asked if she could help him. He said, "Well, if you're not afraid to climb up here, I can sure use some help. Claire didn't hesitate as she knew there wasn't anyone else to help him.

While she was up there, Della saw her and started screaming at her, "Claire! Come down from there! Are you crazy? You can't do that; you're too old to be up there like that. What do you think you're doing?" Della was so upset that she ran out to the street to get away.

When Della came back, Claire said to her, "Why are you so upset? Bob needed someone to help him with that, and I'm the only one here to do that. If I didn't think I could do it, I wouldn't." Della finally calmed down, and Bob and Claire got the tarp on the roof. Claire thought they really didn't know what they were doing, but here again, their adrenalin went to work.

They were finding pillows, sheets and pillow cases, and all kinds of clothing all over the property—on trees, in the mud, and clinging to the debris. They tried to gather up things, thinking they could be laundered, but they couldn't. Bob put up some rope lines, and Della and Claire hung everything on them to dry. By then, the sun was shining and it was warming up. The place looked like *The Grapes of Wrath*.

Bob's generator was acting up, so Bob said he would take it to his mechanic friend and see if he could fix it. He took it over to him and together they got it running, but they weren't sure for how long.

While he was there, he heard about a place that was expecting some generators to arrive by barge in the next day or so. It seemed that the mainland and the other islands had been alerted and came to the rescue immediately, flying some in. The island was receiving help with some of the necessities needed for survival.

Claire and Della were still roaming around when Bob returned.

Then Bob said, "I'll tell you what we'll do, we'll clean out the one garage, where we store the tractors and equipment, and try to bunk in there for now." It was the only garage that had plumbing in it for a three-quarter bathroom, and luckily the garages on that side did not get damaged much, only the garage doors blew off the tracks.

So they all pitched in and cleaned that one out, then they looked around for anything in the wreckage that they could salvage to use for their makeshift living quarters. They had the one box-spring, and they found another one with a mattress that was soaking wet, and they put it in the sun to dry. This one, Claire thought, could be for Della when it dried.

Claire gathered everything she could find that she could put on top of the hard box-spring to form a mattress: blankets, packing quilts, bedspreads, sleeping bags, anything that was capable of being dried and used to soften the springs. They did find enough bedding that could be dried and used. It was very hot and humid, so they didn't need much.

Claire still hadn't heard from her children and of course, there was no way for them to know if anyone had been killed or badly hurt, from all of this. All of a sudden, Claire looked up to see her children running up the driveway toward them. The driveway was all covered with downed trees from the orchard and other debris, so she didn't see them until they were almost at the house.

She was so happy she couldn't stop crying; she almost became hysterical. She was so glad to see them walking and not hurt. They said they had to walk about two miles from where they parked their car because they couldn't get through the roads, as the roads were full of telephone poles and downed trees. They also said their little house had very little damage, but the house where Jerry was living, which was right behind theirs, had received a lot of damage, the roof completely blown off. Since Jerry was in Maui, working on a job, he couldn't reach Claire in any way, and she couldn't contact him.

After Claire found out that they were all OK it made things a little better.

Bob was still having problems with the generator, so the refrigerator that they moved down from the damaged house to the garage, where they were going to bunk, was not working properly. Luckily, they found the stew, which was still good, as they had kept it on ice.

They dug out the barbeque grill from the rubble and set it up near the door of the garage to cook on. They also found some battery lamps that they used for camping and set them up for the night. By nightfall they had two beds set up, plus a table and four chairs, that they found in the rubble, which were only slightly damaged; all of it they picked out of the damaged stuff outdoors. Finally they spotted the sofa from the living room and dug it out, and discovered it was broken, so sweet old Bob wired it together securely enough for them to sit on and moved it into the garage apartment. They also found a pair of broken armchairs and a couple of tables. They didn't have anything to put their clothes in, but they were able to salvage some drawers from the dressers that were damaged, and Claire stacked them all on top of one another to form a dresser; but the drawers would not slide out—they had to lift them up to get what they needed.

Little by little, they had an apartment put together with junk they found all over the property.

Della wanted to go back home, but Bob said to her, "That will not be for quite awhile as there are no planes available. They're using all the flights for FEMA and bringing in suppliers and equipment." So she calmed down a little.

It was not easy sleeping on a pile of blankets and other stuff, especially for poor Bob, being over six foot tall and about a hundred and eighty pounds. He did tolerate it though for a few days until he found a retailer who got in a shipment of mattresses. All of the stores on the island were damaged, and all the mattresses were damaged or soaked.

It was awful not having water to flush the toilets. They were lucky the first few days as Bob had insisted they fill everything with water before the storm, just for that purpose. In a couple of days he had the water lines repaired so that they were able to flush.

The thing that happened that Claire thought was kind of humorous was that every place Bob looked—the rubble, the orchard trees—he found Claire's lingerie hanging on something, and he would come in holding a stick decorated with her panties or bras.

It had been a couple of weeks, and they still had no phone or electricity or drinking water. Claire checked everywhere to find someplace to live, but too many condos had been damaged, and those that were not were reserved for all the people who were brought in to assist in the rebuilding: such as FEMA, officials, insurance adjusters (theirs was from South Carolina), phone and electric repairmen, and others. Some of those people were put up in condos and hotels that were damaged but barely livable. They were arriving from all over, and there were hundreds of them.

But really, Bob and Claire preferred to stay close to their property. Bob went to the planning department to ask if they could convert the garage into living quarters, since there was no place to live. The planning department said, "Whatever you can do for living quarters, you go right ahead and do it. Lucky you have something to convert." So Claire and Bob talked it over, and Bob asked Claire, "Honey, do you think you can draw up and make a livable apartment out of this twenty by twenty-eight-foot garage, adding a bedroom to it since we may need to stay in it for quite awhile, possibly a year or more? We don't have any idea how long it will take to rebuild and find a contractor and materials. Everyone is scrambling for contractors and materials on the entire island." They felt so lucky and comfortable and knew they would be more so when they could convert it. So Claire agreed and knew she could do it.

They were so thankful they were still alive and so thankful for the concern of their friends and for all the packages and letters they were beginning to receive. She was sure all the people on the island felt the same way.

By that time, Della was able to get a seat on the airlines out of Kauai, and she was ecstatic, as were hundreds of other people. Claire and Bob saw her off. They felt glad for her.

They still did not have telephone service yet so the telephone company installed phones near one of the banks for people to use free of charge to call anywhere they needed. The people had to stand in a long line to use them. And the government installed a setup to make river water palatable for drinking. They had to drive down to the river to obtain their quota. It was a big operation.

Jerry had an opportunity to fly home on a private plane from Maui, since there was no communications; he wanted to see that all was OK with everyone. So he was there when she and Bob returned home from the airport.

On the way back from the airport, Claire and Bob had a chance to talk about their future and what they should do. Bob said to Claire, "Honey, what do you think we should do; should we rebuild here or do you think we should look elsewhere, maybe on the mainland someplace?"

Claire looked at him and asked, "Do you want to go back to Oregon where you are from?"

He replied, "Hell no! I didn't mean that. I don't think I ever want to go back there. I thought maybe we should go to the mainland, rent a car, and just travel around and see if there is someplace that we both like."

Claire reached over and kissed him and said, "Darling whatever you want to do I will do, and wherever you go I will follow."

With that he grinned and said to her, "Well, let's get these living quarters built up and if we do decide to go, we'll ask Jerry if he'd like to stay there and look after the orchard for us until we come back. It would save him from paying rent where he is."

Claire said, "That sounds good."

When they returned home, Claire got her paper and rulers out and started drawing up the change for the garage. It didn't take her long. Now they had to find a contractor to help them build it. They finally did find a contractor that Claire knew about. He was not a licensed contractor, but he had done some work for someone that Claire knew, and she and Bob felt lucky he could work them in between his other jobs. Claire and Bob had salvaged some of the windows and other items, and they were able to use them, and that saved them some time and money.

As soon as the phones were working, Claire got on the wire and called Container Home Suppliers in Washington and ordered the cabinets and supplies that they needed to complete the new apartment. They shipped it over pretty fast by barge, and in a couple of months it was completed.

They made the decision to go to the mainland and rent a car and look around to see if they could find something they liked well enough to make the change. They talked to Ed Cates on the phone, and he gave them an invitation to stay at their place in Scottsdale, Arizona, to look around if and when they came over.

In the meantime, Bob had ordered young macadamia trees from the

Big Island, to replace the ones that were gone, and Bob and Claire immediately planted all of them again. Then they talked to Jerry about staying there until they decided what they would do. Jerry was agreeable to that, and in March of the next year, Bob and Claire headed for the mainland on a safari for a new home. And Jerry moved into the garage apartment.

Their first stop was California, to the southern part around Vista. Then they drove to Arizona, New Mexico, Colorado, and parts of Utah. After the tour, they went back to Arizona and visited Barbara and Ed Cates. In talking to them, they suggested that Claire and Bob might like Mexico, as they had lived there once and liked it. So the four of them drove to Baja, California, and checked it out, but Bob wasn't impressed with that area as a permanent place to live.

Then they went back to Barbara and Ed's place in Scottsdale for a few days. Ed offered a suggestion that Claire and Bob might like northern Arizona, as a lot of retired people lived there, and the weather was not as hot and dry as the Phoenix area. So Claire and Bob drove all around the northern part of Arizona and finally came to Prescott.

They rented a motel for a few days to look around, and after not finding anything that Bob was glad to see, they were heading south again when they spotted a little town called Dewey. It looked like everyone owned a horse, and it was all farming country.

They couldn't see any real estate offices at first. Then they spotted a little real estate office sitting way back off the highway, and Claire shouted, "Bob, there's one. Pull over there." So he did.

They went in and there was one person, a man who looked like he had just gotten off a horse. The floors were all wood, and there was an old, shabby sofa against the back wall, and only two desks; one said "Broker" with no one sitting there, and it looked like the other was for an agent. Bob related to the man what they were looking for, and he checked his list and then guided them to a couple of properties that Bob didn't approve of. Finally he said, "You know what, there's a lady that works in this office also, and she's been in this area all of her life, and she knows everyone here. She'll be in tomorrow, and I'm sure she can find what you like."

So Bob told him that they would be back the next morning after breakfast.

The next morning, when they arrived at the real estate office, a very sweet, plump, little gray-haired lady greeted them and said she understood what they were looking for. She had something in mind, but she didn't have the key to the place as yet. She knew the people wanted to sell, but they were out of town at the present time. She said, "They had a couple of offers on the place, but the buyers couldn't come up with the down payment and couldn't get a loan."

Bob spoke up then and said, "If it's what we want, this will be cash—no loans."

The little lady's ears really perked up then and she said, "Let me show it to you. I know how to contact these people, and I'll have the key to show you the house tomorrow."

So she guided them to the property, and as soon as Bob saw it, he liked it. Bob looked at Claire and said, "Honey, this has a double-wide mobile home on it, do you think you can live in a trailer?"

Claire answered, "You know, darling, if you are there I can live anyplace, and I can make it livable."

The next day, the lady took them back to see the interior of the mobile home, and it was very nice inside. It had two bedrooms and two baths and an extra room built on for a family room or "Arizona Room," as they called it, and it was very nice. So they were both happy with the property, and together they decided to buy it.

He told Claire later that he did not expect them to live in a mobile home permanently. As soon as they decided to stay in Arizona, he would build her a nice house. It would be a year or less if they decided to remain in Arizona. Claire could not believe she had found a man who would be so kind and thoughtful. It seemed he became sweeter as time went on, and they seemed to love each other more each day.

Then while the sale was going through and all the legal work, Bob and Claire went back to Hawaii to get things settled with Jerry, but before they left Arizona, Bob decided to plant a garden, thinking it would be all ready when they returned. Well, when they returned to Arizona, there had been a freeze in the weather there in June, and all of the vegetables were frozen and gone. That was disappointing to both of them.

They turned their concentration to furnishing the mobile home and making it more comfortable. Claire went out and shopped for some items. They had decided that they didn't want to put too much money into it as they were not sure if they would stay, but as the days went on, they seemed to like it better, and Bob was happy with it. He had plans to get some cattle and sheep, since they would have four plus acres, and he finally did.

Claire spent a lot of time furnishing the interior, making all the draperies, and traveling to Phoenix to buy the rugs for their hardwood floors (with the help of Barbara Cates of Scottsdale), and Bob worked on the outside landscaping. Finally, they sat down and talked about how they liked it there and if they would like to stay. By this time, they had celebrated a Christmas there, and the house was very comfortable, and they both decided they would like to stay.

There was a piece of property next to theirs, and Claire kept telling Bob he had better buy it before someone built something there that we wouldn't like. He said he was thinking about and would come to a decision.

Bob said to Claire, "Well, I guess one of us will need to go back to Hawaii and have a big yard sale and get rid of all our stuff there, the cars and all." Claire looked at him and said, "Yes, we will, and I think it should be you."

With that Bob replied, "Not me. I don't want to see that place again for a long time." Claire knew he was heartbroken when he saw how the place was devastated by the hurricane and saw all the work he had put into it just blown away.

So in late January of the next year, Claire made plans to go back to Hawaii. She was to sell everything that they had left there except the property and the place where Jerry was living. Before she left, Bob had her draw up plans for their new house, and they found a contractor they were pleased with, who would build it the way Claire drew it up.

When she saw their old place, it brought back memories of when she would come home from work, and she and Bob would grab the pickers and together pick up the nuts and talk about things and plans. The time would go by fast and they would pick up bushel bags of them. The trees they planted before they left Hawaii had grown quite a bit, and she could see that Jerry had taken care of them although he was working hard at his job.

Claire had a huge yard sale, and moved out all of their things they wouldn't need any more except some of the macadamia orchard equipment.

While she was there, Bob called and he said to her, "Honey, I'll have your birthday present for you when you return."

Claire became excited and asked, "What is it, darling?"

And he replied, "It's a surprise for you when you get back here."

After the successful sale was over, and Claire took care of all the loose ends, she headed back to Arizona and to her sweet Bob. He used to say he was her SOB (Sweet Old Bob).

Claire was happy to be back with him; she had missed his loving. She discovered that her birthday present was the acreage next to their property. Bob had purchased it, and she was happy about that.

Things were settling down. Bob purchased two cows (and a couple of sheep because Claire liked lamb meat). He also got some black chickens that had feathers all down their legs. Claire had never seen chickens like that before. She was not sure, but it seemed they were called Cajun chickens. They seemed to love Bob, and they would follow him all over the property. He built a chicken house to match their house exactly and painted it the same color.

After they got everything the way they wanted it, Claire began to get restless and said to Bob, "I think I want to go back to work in real estate."

He said, "OK, but would you want to work for an office, or would you like to open your own office?"

Claire thought a minute and replied," Well, you know I'll need to take the test over here to get my license, so I may as well go for a broker's license and work out of my house."

So Bob said, "Well, you get your broker's license, and we can talk about it then."

Claire did get her broker's license, and Bob said to her, "Now that you have it, why don't we look for an office for you?" Claire was overjoyed. After looking around, they found a nice, adaptable place real close to their house.

Bob gave Claire the money to furnish it. She shopped around for second-hand equipment and made it serviceable. Everyone in the area was happy about the office, as they didn't have one in that area. They even had a write-up in the local paper about her opening.

She needed office staff and started by bringing the sweet, little lady in, the one who sold Claire and Bob their house. Next was Floyd, who was a top salesperson, then Gayle and Diana, who were constantly competing for Floyd's love and kept the office in an uproar. She finally had a staff of seven sales people.

When she had it running good, Bob would stop in to visit her and joke around with the agents; he was a great joker. Before he left, he always asked her what she would like for dinner that night, and then had it prepared when she came home. He was a good cook and liked to cook.

Everything seemed to be going very well, but Claire began to notice that sometimes Bob was not himself, although he never complained. Claire had talked to Bob earlier about making up a living trust because of all the property they had now, but he was not agreeable, saying with all the property his dad had, he never had a trust. Claire said to him, "Yes, but you see what happened when he passed, the state got all of his property." And Bob agreed, but he didn't agree about getting the trust.

Claire was healthy, always taking her vitamins. Bob laughed at her. She always tried to get him to take them and take better care of himself, but he would just laugh at her.

One day he told her that he wasn't feeling too well. He had talked to a friend at the county office, and the man said that he and his wife were taking chelation treatments, and it was helping them. Bob said if it would make him feel better, he would like to take those treatments too, but he would like Claire to go and take them with him. So she agreed. They both went and took the treatments for a long period of time. Claire finished her set of treatments and felt good, but Bob did not feel any better. He took them for a longer period, then stopped.

The same man told Bob that his wife was going to Mexico now and taking treatments, and the treatments were not as expensive down there, and she was feeling better. So Bob decided to go to Mexico. He drove there several times, and the doctor gave him some medications, but they didn't seem to help. When he returned, Claire could see that he was no better and that his disposition was changing. He seemed so unhappy. Sometimes she wondered what the doctor had told him. He wouldn't tell Claire.

Then he began doing strange things that were not sensible or normal for him, and Claire thought it was just because he wasn't feeling well. He sold the cattle and sheep and gave his favorite chickens away. Claire couldn't figure out why, but he wanted to do it.

Bob decided to go to Mexico. He drove down there several times, and the doctor down there gave him some medications and formulas, but it didn't seem to help. When he would return, Claire could see that he was no better, and his disposition was changing. He seemed so unhappy. Sometimes she wondered what the doctor had told him. He would never tell Claire.

One day he came home and announced that he had purchased a motor home. He told her that maybe they could take a trip sometime and he could use it to go to Mexico. They did take some short trips to the lakes, etc., but they never went very far.

He did take the motor home to Mexico. He drove it to California near the Mexican border and parked it in a trailer park. And then he would go by bus to the clinic, which was in Mexico.

He did ask her one day if she would like to go on a trip with him to Oregon, and she was delighted. He said he wanted to show her all of the big things he built there when he was in the construction business.

They went, and he seemed to have a good time, showing her where he was from and all the places and buildings he had built, the gravel company he had owned, and the home and land he had there, which his wife got in the divorce settlement. They had a wonderful trip. Bob would park in very nice wooded retreats, and Claire would prepare the evening meals, and they both watched the little animals and squirrels playing around. Bob seemed happy then and they both felt lucky to have one another.

Then Bob bought a little car that he could tow behind the motor home. It wasn't very long afterwards that he decided he was going to take another trip to Oregon, and Claire asked if she was included on this trip. He answered, "No." This was not like her Bob. While he was on this trip, he had a lot of problems with the little car and had a heck of a time getting back. He was still unhappy with everything.

One day he approached Claire in the driveway and said to her, "I don't want to be married anymore; I can't take it." Claire was shocked because they had had no arguments or any disagreements about anything.

She replied, "Bob, what do you mean?"

"I want a divorce."

She answered, "Bob, when I married you, it was for life. I don't want a divorce, and I am not going anywhere. What brought this on?"

"I don't want to be together anymore; I'll move into the motor home."

"Well, Bob, if that's what you want, alright, but that's not what I want."

Bob moved all of his clothing into the motor home. Claire was very dejected and didn't even feel like going to the office, but she did. She didn't know what to do. He said his attorney would be serving her with the divorce papers in a few days.

Claire said to him, "You know what, Bob, you are forcing me to get an attorney, and I really don't want to; also it will cost you. When she was served with the divorce papers, she retained an attorney.

Oh! It was horrendous for Claire to dig up all the information she needed for the attorney. She was beside herself, never dreaming she would have to go through this.

Claire couldn't figure out why he had changed so much. He was doing mean things to her, which he had never done before. It was like he wanted her to divorce him, like he wanted to get rid of her.

Then she saw a man come to visit Bob in the motor home several times, but she didn't know who he was. She had never seen him with Bob before. Claire discovered later that he was the man to make up the living trust that he had previously objected to.

A few nights passed, and he saw her when she came home from the office and asked her if she would like a glass of wine with him before dinner. She accepted. She joined him in the motor home for the wine. He said he had met a man that made up trusts and that he was considering it, and that he may need to have her sign some things. Claire said OK.

Every couple of nights he would invite Claire to have dinner with him in his motor home. She knew he didn't really want to be alone. She was beginning to think that maybe he was so sick that he didn't want her to have the burden of a sick husband.

One night, he asked Claire if she had talked to her attorney lately, and she said, "Yes, I talk to him all the time."

He then came out with a strong remark, "I'm going to fire my 'GD' attorney." Claire couldn't figure out just what he was upset about.

Bob had the trust made up, and it was a revocable trust, so Claire really didn't know what it was that she was signing. It was like she was completely in limbo from the whole situation. She was letting her attorney handle it all.

This separation went on for a couple more months. One day when Claire invited Bob to dinner to reciprocate his invitations, because he had invited her to his place for dinner several times, he had a sad look on his face and said, "You know what, Honey? I don't like this, do you?"

Claire replied, "Like what?"

"I don't like being out there in the motor home," he said.

"Well Bob, you know I didn't want this in the beginning, and I don't like it."

"Would you let me come back to you?" he asked.

"Of course; I never wanted you to go." He then came around the table and hugged her and left in a hurry to go to the motor home to bring his things back to the main house.

Claire informed her attorney that Bob wanted to reconcile, and the attorney advised her to have Bob sign some agreements before making a change, which she did. After that, Bob had the trust revoked. Claire was not happy with that. She insisted that they both go to their attorney and have another living trust made up the way that she agreed to. So he finally agreed to go with her, and it was all made over, and the first trust was amended.

He also told the attorney that he was going to donate the Hawaiian property to the Hawaiians. When Claire objected to that, he said, "What should I do with it? Do you want it?"

Claire said, "Of course. We've both put too much work and love in that place to just give it away."

So, he told the attorney, "I guess Claire wants it, so she'll have it." And so it was to be.

By that time, his health was going downhill quickly, and Claire knew then why he was so intent on her separation from him. She knew he didn't want her to have to care for him as a sick person and wanted her to leave him alone to pass on.

He said that the doctors in Mexico told him he had a kidney infection, so the next day Claire called Alan in Hawaii and had him ship over the fresh aloe plants, and she scraped them and put them in a blender and made Bob an orange juice drink. She insisted he drink it every day. Finally, when Claire saw he was not improving, she insisted he go to a doctor in Prescott.

He did, and he had to go to several doctors in Phoenix and other cities before they could get a good diagnosis. And of course, Bob wouldn't tell her what the doctors said to him, and he objected to her going with him.

She thought about getting Bob a dog, because she had heard that sometimes a pet could help a sick person. So they began to look for a dog that Bob would like, and they finally found Sara, a cute Australian blue merle healer, and Bob loved her. As a puppy, six weeks old, she would follow Bob all over.

When Claire had been in Hawaii the last time, her boys wanted to give her a trip to Costa Rica for her birthday in February, but she hadn't told Bob as yet.

Anyway, soon after Bob came back to live in the house, Claire was cooking dinner and Bob asked, "Would you like to go on a cruise?"

A very surprised Claire said to him, "Yes, when? The boys wanted me to go to Costa Rica with them in February, it's for my birthday."

Bob said, "Well, I can make the arrangements for March; that should work out."

"Yes, that would be great!

Claire went to Costa Rica, and when she came back, she really looked forward to the cruise. Bob seemed to also, but she could tell he was not his old self. He told her they would take the train to New Orleans and get the ship from there. He did help get his clothing and accessories ready for the trip, but he still acted like he didn't feel well. She could tell, but he would never talk to her about it. When she thought about things later, she figured Bob didn't want to fly to New Orleans because he probably felt too sick to fly.

They left for the cruise and all the way to New Orleans, Bob only wanted to sit by the window of the train and look out at the country. He would keep telling Claire to go and enjoy herself. He did make sure that they enjoyed New Orleans, and they did. Claire thought that when they would get on the ship he would perk up, but he didn't. He only wanted to stay in the stateroom and read and insisted she go and enjoy herself.

Claire knew then that Bob was very ill, and that he knew it and didn't want to tell her. She believed the doctors in Mexico had told him what was really wrong, and he had wanted the divorce so she wouldn't have to put up with a sick husband. He didn't realize that Claire would always take care of him; she loved him that much. She felt that all of this was because he knew he didn't have very long, and he didn't want her to know.

The trip home was an ordeal for him. He was so sick. She tried to keep an eye on him, as he would not complain to her about anything. Claire knew then that all the trouble she had with him about the divorce was because he wanted to save her the trouble of caring for him while he was sick and dying. She believed the doctors in Mexico had told him what was really wrong with him, and he didn't want Claire to know or have her go through that. He didn't realize fully that Claire loved him so much she would always take care of him.

After they returned home, Claire became more insistent about him seeing other doctors. He still refused to let her go with him as she always wanted to. He finally went to a doctor who sent Bob to a kidney specialist, and that is when they discovered Bob had a cancerous tumor on his kidney. Once he called her into the bathroom and showed her a black stool, and she knew that was a very bad sign. He had never alerted her about anything before. She had to call the paramedics several times for him, for some spells, when he had them. Finally they set up a date for surgery to remove the tumor.

Bob had surgery in August and after the surgery, the surgeon told Claire that it would not be long for him, maybe six months if they were lucky. He said they didn't get it all because it had spread—it was the largest tumor on a kidney that he had ever seen. He recommended a cancer specialist for Bob to consult.

Claire was so upset. She called Alan and asked him to come and assist her and go with her to take Bob to see the cancer specialist. She was afraid she would be so upset that she would not hear everything the specialist said. She also needed help in more practical ways. So Alan came to Prescott.

At this point, poor Bob was out of it—he was just turning everything over to whoever was there to help him. Claire and Alan took Bob home and tried to make him comfortable. Claire found a chair that operated electrically and would help him stand upright on his feet, and she bought it for him.

One day she found Bob sitting on the sofa in their bedroom, and the tears were coming down his cheeks. She could tell he was crying. She said to him, "Darling, what's wrong, why are you crying?"

He answered through his tears, "Oh Honey, what will happen to my little dog, Sara?"

Claire said, "Don't worry, darling, I will take care of everything," and she helped him get into the bed. She knew afterwards that he probably was crying because he didn't want to leave her and the life that they had together for the past thirteen years.

Her sweet Bob was slowly getting worse, and soon he could not even go outside. Before long, Claire couldn't handle him any longer. He was too big for her to try and get him in and out of the bed, so she called in the hospice and a twenty-four-hour nurse. He did not want to go back to the hospital, so to please him, she ordered a hospital bed and turned their bedroom into a hospital room. The nurse stayed in the room next to Bob to be close to him, and Claire moved into the guest room which was close enough to hear him if anything went wrong.

Soon he couldn't even talk. He would just make noises and since he was such a big man, it became very hard to turn or move him in the bed. The doctor had told Claire that he didn't know if it would hit his heart first or his brain. She guessed then that it must have hit his brain since he couldn't talk. He tried several times to tell Claire that he loved her, and she could barely make out what he was saying, but she knew.

It broke Claire's heart to see this wonderful man just dwindle away and know that she was going to lose him. He was the one love she had found in her lifetime and now, without her darling Bob, her life seemed to be ending too. She had longed so many years for a love like they had together.

Early in the morning of June tenth, two thousand, her darling Bob slipped away from her forever. God, she felt lost and didn't know what to do, but she knew she had to be strong. Lucky for her the nurse and Alan were still there. Alan was asleep in the motor home, and she ran out there and got him.

After Bob was gone, Claire had the real estate office to think about; but she couldn't get her mind on it. Then she thought about what she was going to do. She could not see staying there so far from her children and grandkids and the property in Hawaii, so she decided she would sell her office and the home and all the property in Arizona. She would take his little dog and move back to their paradise and rebuild the house right where it was when she and Bob were together. She would go from there. She would be closer to Bob there because they had worked together so hard on that property.

Sometimes at night she could still feel her Bob in the bed with her and he would squeeze her and say, "Gotcha, Honey," just like he did when he made love to her. She knew she would never get her darling Bob out of her thoughts, and there would never be another Bob. She was so thankful she had finally found the one sincere love in her life.

She sold the office and their home in Arizona and packed up all their possessions that she and Bob had collected and with his little dog, she moved back to paradise. That was her decision, and she followed through with it. So, with a heavy heart and a very lonesome feeling, she headed back to Hawaii without her love.

She decided that after the house was completed, she would spend her time with her children and grandchildren and doing gardening, painting and writing, and some traveling. She loved to travel and meet people. God, it would be so nice to have Bob with her to do all these things together—he would have loved that. There would never be another Bob...

Claire Gilbert, née Honey Diehl, was born in 1920 in Pennsylvania. Raised by her father and stepmother, she survived a difficult childhood, emancipating herself at the age of fifteen by boarding a bus to Los Angeles, California. She started working when she was barely a teenager, reinventing herself many times over. Her joie de vivre and lack of artifice has translated into an eventful and colorful life during the most remarkable era in the country's history. Claire personifies the guts and charisma of the Greatest Generation, starting from nothing and achieving the American dream. Along the way, she has struggled with poverty, war, natural disaster and heartbreak, but she has forged a successful career, nurtured a family, made many wonderful friends, and found one great love. Claire currently lives in Hawaii where she paints and writes.